THEN WILL THE GREAT OCEAN WASH DEEP ABOVE

THE THIRD BOOK OF THE APOLLO QUARTET

Ian Sales

Whippleshield Books
www.whippleshieldbooks.com
UK

Published by Whippleshield Books

www.whippleshieldbooks.com

ISBN 978-0-9571883-7-2 (limited)
ISBN 978-0-9931417-0-6 (paper)
ISBN 978-0-9571883-8-9 (ebook)

Edited by Jim Steel
Cover by Kay Sales (kaysales.wordpress.com)

Second edition: January 2015

*Therefore, I greatly fear in heart and spirit that as soon as he sets the light of the sun, he will scorn this island—for truly I have but a hard, rocky soil—and overturn me and thrust me down with his feet in the depths of the sea; **then will the great ocean wash deep above** my head for ever, and he will go to another land such as will please him, there to make his temple and wooded groves.*

Homeric Hymn to Delian Apollo
(translated by Hugh G Evelyn-White, 1914)

The Mercury 13
Geraldyne M "Jerrie" Cobb

Janet Christine "Jan" Dietrich	Marion Dietrich
Mary Wallace "Wally" Funk	Bernice "B" Steadman
Jean Hixson	Myrtle "K" Cagle
Sarah Gorelick	Rhea Hurrle
Irene Leverton	Gene Nora Stumbough
Geraldine "Jerri" Sloan	Jane Briggs "Janey" Hart

UP

It is April 1962. NASA arranges a press conference and gets the astronauts all gussied up and puts them on a stage behind a big table in a conference room in Dolley Madison House. There's maybe one hundred reporters in the room but not many men—and that includes the handful on the stage, like the NASA Administrator, Dr T Keith Glennan; and Dr W Randolph Lovelace and Brigadier General Donald D Flickinger, USAF, who started the whole thing when they put a group of women pilots through the astronaut tests.

The reporters ask lots of questions, about the selection process and the testing, and each of the thirteen gives the answers NASA has told them to give. Then a reporter sticks up her hand, Dr Glennan points at her and the reporter says, I would like to ask Mrs Hart if her husband has anything to say about this, and/or her eight children?

They are all as enthusiastic about the programme as I am, Janey Hart says; even the little ones.

How about the others? asks the reporter. Same question.

Suppose we go down the line, one, two, three, on that, says NASA Director of Public Relations Walter T Bonney. The question is: has your husband, or maybe he's just your beau, has he had anything to say about this?

Not all of the astronauts are married, not all of them are courting. When you log thousands of flying hours, there's not much room for cuddles and candle-lit dinners. Those who are married echo Hart's answer—everything back home is peachy, hubby backs her to the hilt, the kids think mom is great.

Geraldine Sloan, Jerri, the year before she was testing top secret terrain-following radar for Texas Instruments, flying B-25s a handful of feet above the waves over the Gulf of Mexico, she leans toward her microphone and says, I don't think any of us could really go on with something like this if we didn't have pretty good backing at home. If it is what I want to do, my husband is behind it, and the kids are too, one hundred percent.

A couple of eyebrows behind the table go up—they all know Sloan's marriage is pretty much over. If not for NASA public relations, Jerri and Lou would have gone their separate ways last year.

There is a shadow hanging over the conference though no one mentions it: the Russians have already put the first man into space, and followed him with a second; and it's going to be a while before the US can follow suit. NASA, however, will have the first woman in space, they're going to make sure of that—even though there are rumours coming out of the Soviet Union they're training a female cosmonaut, some parachutist, not a pilot.

Once the press conference is over, the "lady astronauts" file out and are bussed back to the hotel through the warm Washington air. Jerrie Cobb stares out the window of the coach and she's thinking about flying, about getting into the cockpit of one of those new supersonic jet fighters; while behind her she can hear one of the others wondering if they'll get to keep the Bergdorf Goodman suits they're wearing. They won't let Cobb near a jet fighter, of course; she has ten thousand hours in over two-dozen types of aircraft, but she's never flown a jet. Only men get to fly jets.

But pretty soon she'll be going higher and faster than

any jet pilot.

A week later—they're still using Dolley Madison House, NASA headquarters, as a base of operations—Jackie Cochran joins them. NASA has signed her on as Head of the Astronaut Office, which means she's now in charge of them. Cobb is not happy, she doesn't trust Cochran, she has seen some of the letters Cochran wrote to the other women after they'd finished the first phase of the testing. Cochran's hints about "favouritism", her words that "one of the girls has an 'in' and expects to lead the pack", all the poisonous little turns of phrase Cochran used to present herself as the true leader of the "lady astronauts".

Now it is official.

Cobb knows she was not really the first, Ruth Rowland Nichols underwent some centrifuge and weightlessness testing at Wright-Patterson Air Force Base six months before Cobb was invited to the Lovelace Clinic; but Cobb, she was the real guinea pig, she was the first to complete all three phases of the testing, she was the subject of Dr Lovelace's talk at the Space and Naval Medicine Congress in Stockholm, she appeared in Life magazine.

And it was Cobb and Janey Hart who campaigned for NASA to push ahead with its Mercury programme using women. Cochran has always said, even when she ran the Women Airforce Service Pilots during the last war, she's always said the men go first and the women follow after and take up the slack. But there's no slack here now, all the men have gone out to Korea to fight the Soviets and the Chinese.

Cobb wants to go to Dr Glennan, but Hart argues against it. We were lucky, Hart tells Cobb, we were lucky the pilots they originally picked had to go back to active duty, we were lucky the other men NASA wanted are the kind that won't stay here but have to go off to fight in Korea. You know Jackie has been working to take over right from the start, well now she's done it.

Hart puts an arm around Cobb's shoulders. She drops

13

her voice and adds, But Jerrie, Jackie is an old woman and not in good health. We're going into space, Jerrie. Jackie isn't.

Later, Cobb has to admit there are some advantages to having Cochran in charge. They all get to visit the White House when Cochran arranges a dinner with President Eisenhower and the members of the US Senate Committee on Astronautics and Air and Space Sciences. In evening gowns by Oleg Cassini and Norman Norell, accompanied by husbands or uniformed chaperones—Cobb finds herself on the arm of a young USAF first lieutenant from Texas called Alan Bean—they all sit down to a five-course dinner in the State Dining Room. Cochran and Eisenhower go back years, and every time someone asks a question of one of the astronauts, Cochran jumps in with an answer—and the president just nods and gives his sunny smile. Hart catches Cobb's eye and makes a face, but what can they do? The others, they're too excited about eating in the White House, about the photo session—Cochran has arranged an exclusive contract with Life magazine—before they were led into the State Dining Room. Cobb is thinking about spacecraft and wondering what the Earth will look like from one hundred miles up, and she wants to be the first woman on the planet to see that.

The next day, the astronauts—the press calls them the Mercury 13 now—fly down to Cape Canaveral for a guided tour, in a chartered Douglas DC-6 piloted by Cochran, although they could have all flown there themselves. From the airport they're bussed to the Holiday Inn in Cocoa Beach. That evening, as the sun sinks below the horizon, spraying red and orange across the palms and freeways, the women gather down by the pool, all except Cochran, and in the twilight they sip cocktails and chatter excitedly about the days ahead. It feels like some fevered dream, this group of well-dressed and well-spoken women with their martinis and manhattans and daiquiris, in the sharp heat of the lacquer-clear Florida night, and they're all thinking they're but a stone's throw from Cape Canaveral... A couple of days ago, sitting in a conference room, they were being presented to the world as pioneers, explorers of a new frontier, and they could feel on them the paternal gaze of the NASA meatball on the curtain behind the table. But this... this could be a meeting of the 99s. There's excitement in the voices but the laughter is brittle; the gestures are emphatic and the glasses are being drained faster than usual. Cobb watches the other women for a moment, then looks away. She's standing at the edge of the terrace, before her is the space-dark sea and the moon-bright sand, and she's barely touched the martini someone handed her.

There's a clatter of heels on the concrete, and Hart walks up and stands beside her.

We did it, Jerrie, Hart says. By God, we did it. We get to go way up there, where no man has gone before. Well, no American man anyway.

She flings up a hand, gesturing at the night sky and the stars sparkling like diamonds in it.

Cobb says nothing. When she sees a rocket launch, and a woman atop it, then she might start to relax. But not now, not yet.

Who will be first? she asks Hart. Who do you think?

You mean us or the Russian woman?

No, among us, out of the thirteen of us.

Hart shrugs and takes a sip of her martini. She plucks out the olive, eats it and then flicks the toothpick out onto the beach. You, she tells Cobb, you should be first, Jerrie. You did all this, you put us here.

They both know it's not so simple. Yes, Cobb first handed a list of candidates to Dr Lovelace; but Jackie Cochran put her own names in as well and she paid for all the medical testing, so there's some of the thirteen who think Cochran is the right woman to lead them. And now NASA has offically put her in charge. There's going to be a game of favourites in the weeks ahead, Cobb can see that.

You'll get to fly, Jerrie, Hart assures her. No matter what

15

Jackie does or says, you'll get to fly.

DOWN

Lieutenant Commander John Grover McIntyre leans on the rail, draws on his cigarette, and gazes west toward Hispaniola. Ribbons of sunlight dance across the swell and the sky is heart-achingly blue, but he's thinking about being pulled from the Navy Experimental Diving Unit at the Washington Navy Yard. They flew him to Roosevelt Roads Naval Station, Puerto Rico, on a Grumman C-2 Greyhound, and then three hours cleaving the restless sea in a 65-foot utility boat out to the USS White Sands... and there in the ship's aft dock well is the white torpedo-shape of the Trieste II. As soon as he spots the bathyscaphe he knows what he's doing here 1,600 miles south of home.

He's going to the bottom of the Atlantic Ocean.

As near as he can figure it, they're some seventy-five miles north of San Juan, somewhere above the Puerto Rico Trench, and there's around 27,000 feet of water under the USS White Sands' keel. McIntyre is not happy. The Terni pressure-sphere is only rated to 20,000 feet and he's wondering if the guy running this operation knows that—

Which would be Commander Brad Mooney, commander of the Integral Operating Unit, and all he's told McIntyre is that the USNS De Steiguer found the target weeks ago after ten days steaming up and down the search zone, while the IOU was making test dives off San Diego; and they got to move fast as the deep ocean transponder batteries have a guaranteed life of only one month. No one's said what the "target" is yet, what it is McIntyre's supposed to be bringing up from the sea-bed. The Rube Goldberg contraption Perkin-Elmer have bolted to the front of the Trieste II—he's heard it called a "hay hook" and a "kludge"—looks like it might work, but McIntyre's sceptical, he knows the bathyscaphe; and for something

16

that's as simple as a steel ball hung beneath a float filled with gasoline, she's temperamental and fragile and she knows how to make her commander's life hell. He thought he'd given her up back in 1967, when he transferred out to NEDU but here he is again, two years later, flown in because the bathyscaphe's current commander busted a leg on the journey bringing Trieste II from San Diego to Puerto Rico. So he guesses she's not ready to say goodbye just yet.

McIntyre was all over the bathyscaphe the day before, reminding himself of her systems and workings, and she looks pretty goddamn shipshape, but they need to get her out into the water. They've got a week of fine weather forecast and maybe it will hold. McIntyre holds out a hand and feels the sun beating down on his palm; and there's not a breath of wind, the sea surface is a gelid swell lapping noisily against the hull of the auxiliary repair dock.

Earlier, he spotted a pair of suits lurking about, so he's guessing this is some CIA operation. Maybe the flyboys went and lost another H-bomb, a "Broken Arrow" type thing; or perhaps a Soviet sub sank here, one of their nuclear attack ones, a "Victor". Cuba is only five hundred miles north east, and McIntyre is reminded of October 1962...

He flicks his cigarette out into the sea, checks the Omega Seamaster on his wrist, and then settles his cap more firmly on his head. This is where he gets to learn what he's diving for: the suits have scheduled a briefing. He's looking forward to it, he likes the idea of pulling the CIA's nuts out of the fire.

There's six of them gathered in the ward room, it's hot and the two open scuttles are doing nothing to stir the still air. The two spooks have ditched their jackets and their white shirts don't look so starched now. One has loosened his tie, the other slips off his spectacles every few minutes and polishes them with a handkerchief. Both have buff folders on the table before them. McIntyre and the two bathyscaphe crew, Lieutenants Phil C Stryker and Richard

H Taylor, take seats alongside Mooney, across from the CIA guys.

What do you know about spy satellites? the one with glasses asks.

Nothing, says McIntyre. They're secret, right?

The spook gives an unamused smile. The KH-4B Corona, he says, is what we use to keep an eye on the bad guys, on the things they don't want us to see and we don't want them to know we can see. Let's just say you don't need to know more than that.

He pulls a piece of paper from his folder and slides it across the table. This, he tells them, shows how we get the film down from orbit.

The piece of paper is a diagram in colour: a rocket above the earth, a line of capsules falling from it in an arc and sprouting a parachute, while beneath waits a plane trailing a hook.

We send out a C-130 from the 6549th Test Group out of Hickam AFB and they catch the bucket, says the guy with glasses.

You lost one of them buckets, says McIntyre.

The other spook nods. We think maybe a malfunction kicked it out early, he says. We didn't get a plane in the air in time.

From Hickam? McIntyre asks. Hawaii, right? Dropping it in the Atlantic instead of the Pacific is some malfunction. So now it's below us? In the Puerto Rico Trench? You know that's 27,000 feet deep, right? The Trieste can only dive to 20,000 feet. We go any deeper than that— He forms a sphere with two cupped hands and then suddenly, and loudly, claps his palms together: *crack!*— Deeper than 20,000 feet and we go like that.

The guy with the tie at half-mast answers, It's on a shelf about 19,500 feet down, it's pretty flat and level—

He opens his folder and pulls out half a dozen black and white photographs. The USNS De Steiguer took these, he says, with the camera on the search fish.

He slides the photographs across to McIntyre, who fans them out across the tabletop. The bucket is a circular metal structure, surrounded by a halo of debris. To the right, a light on a cable illuminates the object and throws a pencil line of shadow off the left edge of the picture. The sea-bed looks flat and smooth, like a powdery desert.

It's intact? McIntyre asks.

We think so, the spook says. It hit the sea at a pretty good clip but we think it held together.

And that contraption you've bolted on the front of the Trieste, that's supposed to just scoop up this bucket from the sea-bed? McIntyre asks.

Mooney speaks up: You're in on this late, John. Phil and Dick already ran a bunch of test dives back in San Diego. The hay hook works.

The other spook adds, The USNS De Steiguer dropped a transponder about eight feet from the bucket so it should be easy to find.

McIntyre is not convinced: there's no light down there thousands of feet below the surface, only what the bathyscaphe carries—and her search lights don't illuminate much. He remembers previous dives, sitting in that cold steel ball and looking out at a blurred and ghostly landscape which seemed to stretch only yards in each direction before darkness took over, before reality ran out of substance...

And every time, he felt like an astronaut peering out at that grey sand, gazing out at a world which would kill him in a heartbeat.

UP

The first thing Jackie Cochran does the moment she's settled into her office at the Langley Research Center, the new home of Project Mercury, is send the astronauts make-up from her Jacqueline Cochran Cosmetics range and comprehensive instructions laying out how the Mercury 13 must dress when appearing in public. They're about to go into space, to do something men have never done, and the Head of the Astronaut Office is telling them to keep their seams straight, their hair dressed and to wear powder and lipstick at all times. But none of them complains. Cobb remembers two years ago, approaching Oklahoma City at the end of her non-stop distance record flight from Guatemala City, trying to get out of her flight suit and into dress, stockings and high heels without losing control of her Aero Commander. It's expected of them, it's expected of women.

Proudly displayed on the wall of Cochran's office is the cover of Life magazine with the thirteen astronauts in evening gowns, one of the photographs taken before the dinner with President Eisenhower. And there, in large white letters next to the masthead, are the words "Jackie's Space Girls". Cochran loves it—My space girls, she says proudly. Hart grimaces but won't rise to the bait. Some of the others, the Dietrich twins, Irene Leverton and K Cagle, gather round the framed cover, reaching out to touch the glass, putting fingers to the evening gowns they wore—they didn't get to keep them—and there's laughter and happy compliments, and Cobb sees the group is beginning to fracture.

Cobb knows she will fly, and if it means doing what Cochran tells her to do, then it's a price worth paying.

When Cochran calls the astronauts into her office halfway through their training, five months after they all moved to Langley, Cobb suspects the worse. If she thought the first flight was hers—she was the first to pass the tests, she has the most flying hours, she and Janey Hart did all the campaigning that made this happen—if Cobb expects the first flight to be hers no questions asked... well, there are rumours flying around that say different. This meeting in Cochran's office, it has to be about that.

The thirteen of them enter the room. Cochran is behind

her desk, she doesn't rise to her feet. At her shoulder is Walter T Bonney, the PR director. A few of the women have turned up in flightsuits, fresh from training; some are in slacks. They stand around, eager to hear the news, giving each other speaking glances, and Hart reaches out and gives Cobb a sisterly touch on the arm. That hurts, that Hart could think Cobb will be passed over.

But no. Cochran opens her mouth and out spills a lecture, a rant, liberally dosed with expletives, about the need to keep up standards of dress. No flightsuits in the classroom; make-up at all times unless they're in a cockpit, and even then they put some on before they deplane. She complains she has seen astronauts looking slovenly about the building, and she won't have it. This is not 1943, it is 1963. The engineers and the scientists, a lot of them are men and they expect women to look and behave like women. The women engineers and scientists, they're not role models like the Mercury 13, they're not the reason why this programme exists.

It is a bizarre and filthy-worded tirade, and Cobb can see she is not the only one in the room astonished by it.

Now, says Cochran, visibly calming, I asked you here for another reason. We're about ready to announce who's going to be the first American in space.

If there is a senior astronaut, it's Cobb, but she and Cochran don't like each other, and they'd argue all the time if Cobb weren't so unwilling to speak up, even after all the speechifying which got the thirteen of them here. They all know the score, they all know Cobb deserves the first flight, but there's no real surprise when Cochran says, I've spoken to all your instructors, and I've even been to see dear old Wernher, and we think, we think the first American in space should be... K.

For several seconds, the room is silent.

Cochran puts her hands together and applauds. Well done, K, she says.

The others crowd around Cagle and congratulate her,

hugs and pecks on the cheek. Cobb looks down, feeling like an outsider; she's disappointed, it's heartfelt, a burning sensation deep inside, but she comforts herself with the knowledge that God has something greater for her to do yet. She catches a few sympathetic glances thrown her way, then crosses to Cagle and wishes her luck.

Cagle turns to Cochran at her desk and she says, Miss Cochran, thank you so very much. I'm *your* girl, I believe in you, I trust your judgement in any situation. You have proved we can get what we want, not by pushing, but by winning.

It's no less astonishing an outburst than Cochran's, but at least afterwards Cagle has the grace to look embarrassed. Cochran has a smug expression on her face; Cobb refuses to meet her gaze.

Jerrie, Cochran says, I want you as backup for K.

Only if I get the next one, Cobb replies.

Cochran glowers, she opens her mouth but closes it without speaking. She looks down at her desk. You get the next one, she says in a clipped voice, I had you down for the next one, so don't you go playing games with me.

Later, Cobb thinks it may not be 1943 but it is *like* it. The men have all gone to war and the Rosie the Riveters are back in the factories, back "picking up the slack". There's no WASP because women can't fly jet fighters or jet bombers, the F-103 and F-107, the B-49 flying wing and supersonic B-59; but women have once again stepped out of the kitchen.

Now that the schedule is set for the first two flights, the nature of the training changes. Cagle and Cobb are busier than ever. In Cobb's Aero Commander, they fly down to the McDonnell Aircraft plant in St Louis to have a look at the Mercury spacecraft. It's a frighteningly small vehicle in which to brave the unknown dangers of space, but Cagle fits in it with room to spare. She'll be wearing a pressure suit, of course, one made to measure. The two of them look in through the hatch and Cobb tries to imagine some hefty jet fighter pilot squeezed into its tight confines.

It's really happening, Jerrie, isn't it, says Cagle.

Cobb nods, though she's wondering why there's no control stick.

They alternately spend hours in a mock-up of the capsule, learning the function of every switch and dial, not that there are many of them, far less in fact than on the instrument panel of Cobb's Aero Commander. How to use the periscope, how the environmental control system works, operating the earth-sky camera... They practice on the Air-Lubricated Free-Attitude Trainer, the Multiple-Axis Space Test Inertia Facility, the egress trainer, even flights on the "vomit comet" to experience weightlessness...

This first flight into space by an American will only be a suborbital hop. The Russians have put two men into orbit, but NASA wants to play it safe. The next flight, Cobb's flight, will be orbital...

On hearing this news she knows that God is still looking out for her.

DOWN

It is just past 2200 hours by the time they've filled the float with 67,000 gallons of aviation fuel, loaded thirty-two tons of steel shot, checked out all the onboard systems, and loaded the plot onto the NAVNET computer. McIntyre is on the fairwater deck abaft of the sail, at ease as the bathyscaphe rolls gently in the swell. He leans against the mast, the US flag snapping above his head, and pines for a cigarette—but with all this gasoline beneath his feet, it's not safe. Hollow knocks and the murmur of conversation, evidence of industry in some abyssal realm, echo up the access tube. The USS White Sands sits on station two hundred feet away, far enough not to be caught in the conflagration should the Trieste II's aviation fuel ignite.

Somewhere behind the auxiliary repair dock lies the USS Apache, but her running lights are occluded. There's a fifteen-foot boat containing a pair of sailors a dozen feet away, and a sailor up on the bow of the Trieste II checking out the steering thruster there. It's a warm breezy night, a river of stars running across a black sky, a velvety blackness that shrouds the planet from horizon to horizon, blending softly into the slowly rolling waves. It'll be blacker down below, and it'll also be cold. Those steel walls may protect against the pressure, but they're no defence against the chill. Not even all the equipment in the pressure-sphere, not even three guys in close proximity for hours, can stave it off.

They don't call it the abyssal zone for nothing. *The abyss.* Eternal darkness, temperature 35º to 37º Fahrenheit, pressures up to five tons per square inch. Yet there is an even deeper zone, the hadal zone, down in the trenches, past 20,000 feet, where the pressure reaches seven tons per square inch. There are only a handful of places on the planet that qualify—and the Puerto Rico Trench is one. If the bucket from that spy satellite had not landed on a shelf, but sank all the way to the bottom...

He remembers the French Navy descended to the floor of the Puerto Rico Trench five years ago, and their Archimède could maybe have retrieved the bucket. Back in 1960, the old Trieste, she went all the way down to Challenger Deep, the deepest part of the earth's oceans, 36,000 feet beneath the surface. But the Trieste II is not the same boat, she doesn't have the same pressure-sphere from that record-breaking dive, she doesn't have the same float, the same systems. She's a real operational submersible now, though she can no longer go as deep.

Abruptly, the sea about the bathyscaphe lights up, a ghostly radiance beneath the surface, as if the water itself has turned luminescent. McIntyre leans out and looks down, and he can see the flank of the Trieste II curving away beneath the waves, pale and spectral, blurred in the softly stirring water, a phantom whale basking in the night sea. He shivers at the thought—they're only testing the bathyscaphe's search lights, but the fancy makes something unearthly of it.

Ten hours it took them to ready the Trieste II, after they had flooded the USS White Sands' aft dock well and towed the bathyscaphe out into the Atlantic; and soon they'll be spending hours in the depths of the ocean, hunting for the bucket from this spy satellite. A long day— No, a long *night*. McIntyre was glad to give up nights like this when he transferred to the Navy Experimental Diving Unit, but he has to admit that right now he's feeling a little of the old excitement.

He checks his Seamaster, they're scheduled to dive at 2230, around twenty minutes from now. The water about the Trieste II suddenly turns black, and one of the sailors in the boat shouts something but McIntyre misses it. The boat's outboard fires up with a cough and a roar, and then burbles away throatily. The boat bounces on a wave, its bow slapping down onto the sea surface.

Whatever the problem was it's gone, sir, says the sailor from the steering thruster.

He's standing by the small boat standoff now, hanging onto the rail, as the boat noses in close to the bathyscaphe.

Right, McIntyre replies, we'll be all done below in about ten minutes.

The boat is near enough so the sailor scrambles into it. The prow swings away and the boat moves out to a position thirty feet away, its outboard still snorting and gurgling. McIntyre gives a wave, then enters the sail and climbs into the access tube. He shuts and locks the hatch above him, then descends the ladder to the pressure-sphere. Stryker and Taylor turn round and look up at him as he appears, and he's struck anew at how small the sphere is and that he's going to have to spend maybe six or seven hours in a space four feet by four feet square and five feet nine inches high. With two other guys.

All set? he asks.

Taylor nods and then speaks quietly into the mike of the headset he is wearing. McIntyre worms through the hatch, then he and Stryker swing it closed and seal it.

Flood the access tube, McIntyre orders.

He peers through the window in the hatch and watches as water splashes against the thick glass and quickly climbs up it. McIntyre settles on the low stool beneath the hatch, hands on knees, and says, I guess this is it. Phil, flood forward and aft water ballast tanks, let's go see what it's like down there.

Stryker is pilot for this dive and Taylor is on sonar duty. McIntyre's handling the navigation, which for the moment is straight down. And then they'll have to creep around on the sea bed 19,500 feet below, hunting the deep ocean transponder dropped next to the bucket because the bathyscaphe descends in a spiral.

He picks up the underwater telephone handset and informs the USS White Sands that the dive has commenced. See you in the morning, he says.

He puts the handset down and thinks, this is not diving. He's wearing his khakis, he's bone dry and will remain that way, and the nearest he'll get to the water is looking at it through a window four inches in diameter and 5.9 inches thick. He's been down to a simulated 1,000 feet in the NEDU pressure chamber, and spent a week there; he's dived to 600 feet in the North Atlantic, and spent six days in decompression afterwards. The chipmunk-voice from breathing helium-oxygen, air so thick it's a struggle to pull it into his lungs... 260 psi... 18 atmospheres... Ascend to the surface too fast and the bends is the least of his worries.

Sitting in this steel ball is not real. The sea has been a part of his life for decades, he works in it, it's something he can touch and feel and in which he can immerse himself, it's something he can become a part of. But this, there's an air of falsity to it, experiencing the water mediated by technology and cold steel, separated from it. He doesn't feel like a visitor to this submarine realm, he feels like an invader. Now, belatedly, he realises why he joined NEDU, why he turned his back on the Trieste II and walked away from her.

Strange, then, that he should only discover this by returning to her.

UP

Cobb lies on her back in the Mercury capsule she has named Destiny and waits patiently for the countdown to begin. It's been over three hours since they bolted the hatch but she knows patience, she's been in situations like this before. Not lying on her back in a pressure suit, of course, though she has done this in simulations; nor those long, silent and black hours in the sensory deprivation tank at the Oklahoma City Veterans' Hospital three years ago—and when she heard some of the other lady astronauts spent even longer in the tank than she did, she wanted to do it all over again. No, her mind is drawn to the time she flew across the Caribbean through burning blue skies for Fleetway, the time the engine of the T-6 she was delivering to Peru went "pop" and threw oil all over her canopy and more oil seeped into the cockpit, over her instruments and herself. Though Jack Ford was there flying alongside, insisting she ditch, she prayed she'd make it safely to land. And so she did. She's always known God is there for her, that these things happen to her because He makes them happen and He brings her through them.

Remembering that flight, she thinks of Jack, who passed eight years ago, he'd directed her into a landing at Montego Bay International Airport and told he'd loved her. And for two years they had shone so brightly together.

She can hear the blockhouse and the control centre speaking to each other in her helmet headset, but she tunes it out. The gantry has been rolled back and she can see blue sky through the capsule's window. She recalls the excitement she felt when she watched Cagle's Mercury-Redstone 3, America, lift from the launch-pad, rising up through a pale and hazeless Florida sky on a column of fire and thunder, such a pure and wonderful sight. Cobb doesn't feel that thrill now, she is focused on her upcoming mission; she feels only a need to get everything right, to show Cochran and the others that she deserves to be right here right now.

The delay drags on. Through the periscope she can watch grey waves scudding across the Atlantic; in a mirror by the window, she sees the grey blockhouse. Below her, she hears pipes whine and creak, and then everything shakes and bangs as the ground crew check the engines' gimbal mechanism. She thinks about the new president's speech back in June—after Cagle's flight President Kennedy was talking to Congress and he said they should set as a national goal "landing an American on the Moon and returning them safely to the Earth before ten years are up", and she's already thinking past this flight. She hasn't even been into space yet but that's what she wants: to be the first American to walk on the Moon's surface.

The order comes through to top off the lox tanks. This is it. The countdown is finally going ahead. Minutes later, Cobb hears an infernal thunder as the main engines light and the hold-down clamps release with a decisive thud. The rocket begins to rise, slowly, ponderously, balanced atop its roaring pillar of flame. The top of the gantry slides past the window. Cobb offers up another silent prayer, this time one of thanks. She has much to be grateful for and she knows it—she was not first, but the Russians beat America to that, anyway. But she will beat the Russian record for number of orbits about the Earth.

The Mercury-Atlas rolls and shudders a little. Forty-eight seconds have passed, the rocket hits max-Q and the capsule vibrates, the dials and gauges before her blur. She wills herself to remain calm, none of this is unexpected,

Cagle remarked on it happening during her flight. But that noise, that hellish roar, and the G-forces pressing her down into her seat, it makes it all *real*, this is no simulation. Oh this is what she wanted, this is what she prayed for—she feels such a sense of peace, despite the shaking and the demonic clamour and the weight upon her.

Twenty-four seconds later, the vibrations abruptly cease, the ride is smooth and clear and Cobb knows she is at last reaching for the heavens. After a minute, the booster engines cut off and the G-forces drop back to one as the boosters fall away. The sustainer engine continues to fire and the Gs build up once again, pushing Cobb back into her seat. The sky outside the window is black, and she says as much to Hart, the flight's capsule communicator.

Cabin pressure holding at 6.1, she adds. Coming up on two minutes, fuel is 101-102, oxygen is 78-102, Gs are about six now.

Reading you loud and clear, replies Hart. Flight path looked good.

The jettison rockets on the escape tower fire, she sees it tumble away, and relays the fact to mission control. Capsule is in good shape, she reports.

Roger, you're going for it, Jerrie, says Hart. Twenty seconds to SECO.

The sustainer engine cuts off as programmed, and Cobb is no longer pressed hard into her seat, it's almost as if she's falling forward. She relaxes her arms and her hands float up to hang before her. She starts to smile: *zero-G*. She made it, she's in orbit, she's above the sky. The capsule turns around and she sees the curve of the Earth below her, it's so very blue and it glows and it's streaked with clouds; and she can't help saying, Oh the view is tremendous.

And there's the booster, she can see it tumbling away, glinting as sunlight flashes from its white sides, a pencil of brightness against the blue, falling back to Earth, unable to escape as she has done.

You have a go, Hart tells her, for at least seven orbits.

29

Cobb closes her eyes, clasps her hands before her and bows her head as much as she is able in the helmet. She reflects on the glory of God's creation and her current heavenly perspective upon it, she thinks of the part He has played in her life, she thinks of everything she went through, everything she did, to be here in orbit, the second American, the second woman, in space, and the first American to travel about the Earth 160 miles above its surface.

I'm coming back, she tells God silently. This is my first visit but it will not be my last.

She may have to fight Cochran for a second or third flight, or even more, but she will prevail. He will make sure of that.

DOWN

The trail ball, hanging thirty-five feet beneath the Trieste II's keel, tells them they've reached bottom, so McIntyre orders some ballast dropped to give them neutral buoyancy. Taylor is busy trying to get a signal on the Straza Industries Model 7060 deep ocean transponder interrogator from any of the dots, but he's having no luck. McIntyre kneels and peers out through the window—there's not much to see, only the expected blurred and powdery sand of the bottom, tan shading to grey and then black thirty feet away at the limits of the search lights' radiance. If there's life down here, he can't see it—and he tries to imagine what could survive with a pressure of four tons per square inch pressing on skin and eyeballs, compressing internal organs and cells...

Hey, wait a minute, he says.

He's just seen something, a dark shape looming in the blackness on the edge of the light from the search lights. He can't tell what it is—it's not the wall of the trench, they're more than half a mile from that; and another three hundred yards from the drop-off to the Puerto Rico Trench's true floor.

You got anything on the sonar? he asks Taylor.

It's unlikely: the minimum range on the sonar is thirty yards, so anything close enough for him to see is not going to be on its screen.

Got what? says Taylor. Hey, that's strange. Multiple contacts. They just kind of appeared.

But McIntyre is still trying to figure out what it is he's looking at. He lifts a hand and signals for Stryker to use the bow thruster to swing the bathyscaphe to port, and the sea bottom beneath the pressure-sphere rolls smoothly away to one side, the undulations seeming to propagate like waves across stationary sand.

Give her one third ahead on the centreline motor, he says.

The bottom current is about a quarter knot, but it's pulling the bathyscaphe to starboard, so Stryker compensates.

Something vertical and sheer and flat looms out of the darkness.

Full stop, McIntyre orders, hold us steady.

It's the hull of a ship, a tall slab of darkness covered in lumpy streaks of red and brown, rendered in washed-out greyish pastels by the Trieste II's search lights. McIntyre can see a line of portholes, black circular maws in the steel.

Take us up about sixty feet, he says, and reel in the trail ball to fifteen feet.

What you got? Stryker asks.

It's a ship, replies McIntyre. Looks like some kind of freighter.

They are above the gunwale now, and light from Trieste II spreads across an area of deck, revealing the dark shafts of cargo hold hatches, ventilators covered in knobbly lines of rust laid one upon the other like wax on a candle, and bollards mysteriously clean and untouched. He briefly wonders what it would be like to swim through the shattered corpse of this ship, to eel in and out of the gaping hatches, explore her passages and compartments by flashlight—but that's nearly 600 atmospheres out there. The muted reds and oranges and browns and greens of whatever it is that covers the steel, the depth and richness of it, the wax-like runnels hanging from the rails and yardarms, he's guessing this ship has been down here for more than a couple of decades. He's not surprised it's not on the charts—who would look for wrecks this deep?

I'm getting more, Taylor says.

More what? asks McIntyre.

More sonar contacts. Looks like there's a whole damn fleet down here.

McIntyre doesn't understand. The bottom should be clear here, the USNS De Steiguer never mentioned any wrecks, nor did the photographs she took with her search fish show any.

What the hell is going on? he demands. We're still on the plot, right?

He checks the NAVNET computer himself and yes, they're still within the search triangle they plotted back up on the surface, and though Taylor has yet to find dot zero using the Straza, they can't be all that far from it.

McIntyre can see the freighter's superstructure, what's left of it, most of it has collapsed into itself leaving only a tall triangle of steel at one corner, jagged and thick with those streaks of rusty brown, its edges fading into blurred darkness. The rail passes below the pressure-sphere and now there's darkness beneath—

No, McIntyre can see something else spearing up out of the blackness at the limit of the bathyscaphe's search lights. It's no ship but it looks man-made. He stares at it, trying to make sense of the shape, of the play of darkness and shadow. It's some kind of fin, a thin vertical triangle... and beyond it another triangle and beneath both what looks like a narrow cylinder...

He orders Stryker to release some of the gasoline, and

they sink until the echo sounder tells them they're 50 feet above the bottom. McIntyre can see what it is much better now, it glows in the bathyscaphe's search lights. The cylinder depends from the rear of a boat-shaped hull, and he's still puzzled until he realises the two flat stubs on the top of the hull are all that remain of wings. The shape swims into focus, the cockpit, the nose and its ball turret—

An airplane, he says. It's a goddamn airplane. What the hell is an airplane doing down here?

What sort of airplane? asks Stryker.

A flying boat, McIntyre replies, a Martin PBM, I think.

He sits back from the window and rubs one palm up and down his cheek. Damn it, he says, it's like a goddamn junkyard out there, we'll never find the bucket in this. And I'm not risking finding our way through it on the bottom. Phil, drop some more shot, let's go up to about 100 feet, then we'll be clear of the wrecks and maybe we can see where we're going.

But he's still worried they have yet to get a signal from the zero dot and he hopes it doesn't mean the battery on it has gone dead. Because their mission has just become a thousand times more difficult, now they've discovered the bucket landed in some abyssal graveyard of ships and planes...

And that prompts a thought—Bermuda is due north of here and Miami north-west and San Juan due south, and that puts this stretch of the Puerto Rico Trench firmly within the triangle formed by those three places...

UP

Cobb reaches up and unlatches the hatch, struggling in the inflated spacesuit to work the mechanism. She unfastens her seat harness and pushes herself up. Gently, she floats from the spacecraft, through the open hatch and...

Her previous flight could not compare. Then she saw the

Earth through a tiny window, but *this*... She hangs in space, the inflated bladder of the spacesuit forcing her arms out from her sides, and she's uncomfortably warm but she ignores it. Below her curves a cerulean plain—she can see from horizon to horizon, she can see the Earth is a globe, a jewelled globe hanging in Creation. She feels a sense of ineffable serenity steal over her, the same peace she feels deep in her heart when she kneels before the altar in her Oklahoma City apartment. The presence of God is palpable, His handiwork is plain in all she can see, and the joy of it threatens to bring tears to her eyes.

She reaches out but it proves too tiring to keep her arms up before her. She wants to hold the Earth in her arms—she knows it is safe in God's hands, but she wants the world to share her awe, her love of God, the purity of purpose she now feels. She floats there beside the Gemini capsule, basking in the light of Creation, a world unto herself, and she feels the nearest to God she has ever felt. It is all the more heartfelt because she is lucky to be here—

Her Mercury flight was a success and she was celebrated for it. Like Cagle before her, there was no ticker-tape parade but she got to meet President Kennedy. And Jackie too, of course. For a while, Cochran—magnanimous in the reflection of Cobb's glory and what it said about her management of the astronaut corps—was even complimentary: I knew you were the right one for this flight, she told Cobb.

But there were another eleven astronauts to fly before Cobb got a second flight, and even then Jean Hixson and Gene Nora Stumbough found themselves with no Mercury spacecraft available. Which gave them priority on flights in the Gemini programme, the new two-person spacecraft. Cagle, of course, commanded the first flight, with Stumbough beside her, but Cobb is commander of this second one, Gemini 4, and Hixson is sitting in the left-hand seat...

Cochran has looked after her charges well, even Cobb

has to admit as much. When Cobb asked Max Faget to add a window to the Mercury capsule, Faget said it was impossible, the weight penalty was too much. But Cochran made calls and marshalled her contacts, and pretty soon Faget changed the design. What Cochran wanted, Cochran got; and what Cochran's "space girls" wanted, Cochran got. The men are away fighting and the women go up into space, and thanks to Jackie Cochran the Mercury 13 are treated like real pioneers, like astronauts.

Someone is talking to her. Cobb blinks and tries to focus.

It is Hixson: Jerrie, they want you to come back in now.

Back in?

Back in.

A minute longer, Cobb replies, please.

Mission Control say you have to come in now, Jerrie.

Hixson's worry is audible—it is enough to remind Cobb of her mission, of what she was sent up here to do. She doesn't want to leave, she wants to stay out here. The pure freedom of it is intoxicating, she is mistress of her own destiny, beholden to none, it is a tiny echo of this freedom Rosie the Riveter must feel. It is surely what God intended for her, to experience this, to see the entire Earth in its glory rolling sedately beneath her.

You still have two and a half more days to go, says Hixson.

I know, Cobb replies, I'm coming.

She takes hold of her umbilical with both hands, and uses it to turn herself about until she faces the capsule. Pulling herself hand over hand along the golden rope, her hands aching from the stiff gloves, her forearms burning with strain. This is so much harder than flying a four-engined bomber, that B-17 she flew to Paris when she was twenty-two. She nears the open hatch of the spacecraft.

Okay, ready on top, says Hixson.

Now I can enter, says Cobb. This is the saddest moment of my life.

It is a struggle to get herself back into her seat. The

35

inflated spacesuit restricts her flexibility and though she hangs onto the rim of the hatch, she can't swing her hips to get her legs inside. She lets go with one hand and tries again, her legs stiff and immobile and in they go but now her grip is beginning to slip… She's standing on the seat, she slides her feet below the instrument panel, her rear is on the seat now and she reaches down to fasten her harness. She's breathing heavily from the exertion by the time she's buckled into her seat and the hatch above is shut and locked. She's still feeling stunned from the experience of floating alongside the spacecraft, the freedom of it, the *oneness*, the revelatory sense of it all.

The spacecraft is coming up on Carnarvon now and they can once again talk to the ground. Though Cobb is commander, she has yet to recover fully from her EVA so Hixson reports in:

We are back inside the spacecraft. We are repressurised to five psi.

Roger, understand, says capcom. How are you feeling?

Everybody's fine, says Hixson, feeling great.

Capcom requests battery readouts, and Hixson obliges. The numbers flowing back and forth between the spacecraft and the ground remind Cobb of her situation, act to centre her in this ejection seat in this capsule the size of a Volkswagen Beetle, causes the wonder she felt out there to recede so it no longer overwhelms her. She hears capcom say:

We're going to give you a go for 6-4. I'll update a 4-4 load for you with manoeuvre and 6-4 without manoeuvre time.

Cobb speaks before Hixson can answer: We are ready right now.

Okay, says capcom, transmitting a TR.

Got it, says Cobb.

Okay, we are ready to copy your times.

Ready to go.

Capcom says, 4-4: 153. 3 + 18. 21 08 57. 3 + 00. 8 + 43.

Hixson reads back capcom's figures, and the business of powering-down the spacecraft's manoeuvring system to conserve fuel for their remaining time in orbit provides a routine Cobb can use to focus on the here and now. She looks up from the instrument panel and sees the Jacqueline Cochran Cosmetics Company Perk-Up Stick back-up commander Wally Funk has taped there as a joke; and she peers through the window in the hatch before her and now they're in darkness she can see the continents of the black Earth below patterned and limned in lines of light. It is even more jewel-like than the Earth in daylight, but the hand of Man is written across it in that tracery of artificial light and she feels perversely disappointed that God's creation should be spoiled so...

And yet she would not be right here right now, 170 miles above it all, if it were not for Man's ingenuity.

DOWN

This is weird; this, he can't think of an explanation for it. The USNS De Steiguer's search fish took photographs of an abyssal desert, a sea-bottom clear of rock formations and life, just an endless expanse of grey-tan soft and floury sand. And now the Trieste II floats above a graveyard of ships and planes, different ships, different planes, passing in and out of the globe of light the bathyscaphe has brought down with her from the surface. Though McIntyre can only see out to thirty feet in the light from the search lights, the darkness beyond seems to possess a texture hinting at yet more wrecks. He speculates maybe some current swept the ships and planes here into the trench, but he's more angry than curious— No, maybe "angry" is too strong; he's thinking how are they going to find the bucket given the zero dot isn't responding to the Straza and there's all this metal littering the ocean floor.

If the plot on the NAVNET computer is to be believed,

they can't be too far from the bucket. They've been down here over two hours now, the chill has seeped through the steel of the pressure-sphere, he's shivering and they've covered no more than two nautical miles. No one expected them to descend right on top of the bucket, but maybe a few hundred feet away wasn't too much to hope for—

I have one of the dots, says Taylor. Number three.

McIntyre consults his plot. They're about 2,000 feet away, but if they follow a line between dot #3 and where they think the zero dot is... well, maybe they'll find the bucket. Now they have some data, some idea of their relative position, it's going to be a hell of a lot easier. McIntyre remembers the photograph from the search fish and he hopes the bucket is far enough from any wrecks to give a clear sonar contact.

They drive toward dot #3, passing over more wrecked ships, more cracked fuselages of planes, and McIntyre peers out through the window at these shadowed shapes in the depths and he feels a chill more profound than that brought on by the cold abyss through which the bathyscaphe propels herself. Pensate profunde, he thinks; but now he doesn't want to think too deeply about anything except the mission objectives, about finding the goddamned bucket and heading up to the sunlight and air and the beating rays of the sun.

The sterns of ships drift by, fading into and out of the light, their names clearly legible on scarred and discoloured transoms: Cyclops and Cotopaxi and Sandra and Marine Sulphur Queen... And spread all about, the warped and broken bodies of aircraft: a C-54 Skymaster... a Constellation or maybe a Super Constellation, its livery unrecognisable... a C-119 Flying Boxcar... and even a jet, a Boeing 707— no, he can see a USAF roundel, a KC-135 then...

When the Straza tells them they're within six feet of dot #3, Stryker puts the Trieste II on a course due north, compensating for the bottom current, and they drive forward at one knot. The echo sounder tells them every time they pass over a wreck, but they're staying well above them and they've shortened the trail ball cable so it won't snag, McIntyre is keeping watch through the window for masts or funnels or anything they might hit or catch. The sonar at least is working beautifully, with each ship and plane showing up clearly on the screen, and now the contacts are starting to thin out a little, not just hundreds of feet apart but hundreds of yards. And as they sail over one more freighter, with a complex and tangled arrangement of derricks half-collapsed across her main deck and streaked with wax-like runnels of brown and red, McIntyre thinks maybe one day someone should come down here and explore this place thoroughly.

As the wreck slips beneath the pressure-sphere, McIntyre orders Stryker to reduce speed, and he can now see clear uninterrupted sea-bottom out to the thirty-foot limit of the search lights. As he watches, the sphere of light to port appears chopped off, as if a chord has been cut from it and it's a second or two before he realises what he's seeing is the edge of the shelf.

The bucket should be somewhere around here, he thinks; it's not going to be easy to find without the deep ocean transponder working, but at least the bottom is clear and if they take their time they should be able to cover the search area. So they inch forward at half a knot, Taylor bent over the sonar, and McIntyre staring out through the window at the abyssal waters, both in their own way passing their searching gaze over the undulations of the ocean floor.

A shadow flutters in the bottom current off to starboard, just on the edge of the search lights, and McIntyre at first takes it for sea-bottom flora... before he remembers that down here, 19,500 feet below the surface, there's no light and so no plant-life. He orders Stryker to swing the Trieste II to starboard and the bathyscaphe creeps up on the dancing swaying living thing. As they near it, McIntyre sees it is a strip of nylon webbing attached to a piece of bent metal, and it looks fresh, like it hasn't been down here very long. Debris from the bucket, he decides; it's debris from the bucket, some piece of it that broke off as it sank. And he knows they're near their target now, it's somewhere around here, hidden by the darkness, invisible beneath the blackness that presses down around them at four tons per square inch...

And though they've been down here now for over five hours, he's thinking it won't be much longer before he gets to see the sun once again.

UP

After disengaging from the Agena, mission control tells Cobb and Gorelick they have a new target for them to rendezvous. The Gemini 10 spacecraft is in an orbit with an apogee with 167 miles, but now they have to get higher and meet up with an object at 240 miles. Capcom is being cagey and won't divulge what the object is, Cobb thinks it might be the Agena from Gemini 8 but she thinks that's in a much higher orbit.

When she asks capcom just says, We're not at liberty to discuss it at this time.

It's been over a year since her flight on Gemini 4 and her EVA. Cobb was the first American to spacewalk, but it was another record the Russians beat them to. She has learned to be resigned about it. There's still the Moon, beckoning silver in the sky every night, and she prays each day for the opportunity to tread its airless seas of grey dust. Gemini 10's mission is a step toward that dream, they are up here to practice the rendezvous techniques which will be required for a flight to Luna.

And now the Gemini spacecraft is in the higher orbit, their target is on the radar, and the rendezvous will have to be by eye—but even then capcom won't say what it is. They're close enough to make out what they're aiming for, but Cobb still can't tell. A satellite? It looks a bit like an Agena, a bright cylinder with a nose cone. But it is devoid of markings, and without those it's impossible to judge size or distance.

Gorelick fires the thrusters to bring the Gemini spacecraft in phase with the rendezvous target, and twenty minutes later fires them again to put them on the same orbital plane. Cobb is busy on the computer, calculating an intercept trajectory, and once she has the figures, she puts a hand to the joystick between the two seats. Gorelick reads out the range to the target and the range rate, the difference in velocity between their spacecraft and their target.

What's R dot? asks Cobb, staring intently at the approaching target.

Eighty-three feet per second, replies Gorelick.

What should it be?

About seventy.

I'm going to brake.

Range is two miles. You've got sixty-five R dot at two miles.

The spacecraft draws closer. Though they have simulated such manoeuvres, and this is their second rendezvous of the flight, it still requires intense concentration and a delicate hand on the controls.

Twenty-nine R dot, range 0.8 miles, says Gorelick.

R dot is now eleven, says Gorelick, eleven still, holding eleven... nine... seven... 700 feet... 600... holding 600 feet...

Cobb brings the Gemini spacecraft alongside the target, matching its velocity, and now they've rendezvoused she gets her first proper look at it. It's definitely not an Agena target vehicle. She estimates it's around twelve feet long, much shorter than the Agena's twenty feet; in shape, it's a short cylinder topped by a long cone with a rounded tip. Cobb has no idea what it is. Man-made certainly, but she cannot tell if it is American or Soviet.

We're here, she tells capcom. Are you going to tell us

what it is?

There is a moment of silence.

It's secret, whatever it is, says Gorelick.

Capcom says, I need you to look in your checklists binder, right at the back.

Puzzled, Cobb reaches for the checklists floating from a hook on the instrument panel and flips through the binder. The last page should be the postlanding checklist, but another has been added, and she reads it with mounting disbelief. She shows the page to Gorelick and says, Look at this.

According to the $3^3/8$ by 8 inch card, the vehicle they have rendezvoused is a Corona KH-4B spy satellite. They are also instructed not to mention this over the radio, but to refer to the target as the "alternate Agena".

Acknowledge, please, says capcom.

It's an alternate Agena, says Cobb obligingly.

Gorelick looks at Cobb and raises her eyebrows. For a moment, they stare at each other, at their faces framed within their white pressure helmets. They're wearing helmets because firing the manoeuvre thrusters shakes up the interior of the spacecraft, throwing dust and lint and small debris up into the air, and they need to keep their visors shut until it settles back down. They're not wearing make-up, no astronaut ever has done so in space, and even Cochran stopped whipping that particular horse, especially after she sold her controlling shares in the Jacqueline Cochran Cosmetics Company back in 1966. It's taken six years, eleven Mercury flights and eight Gemini flights, but they're no longer "astronettes" or "space girls", they're *astronauts*. They're the only Americans who have flown in space, and they've been beating the Russians in endurance flights for the past three years. There are some advantages to having a women-only astronaut corps, even the scientists and engineers say as much.

They're not front-page news any more, and that suits

them just fine because they're just doing a job, something they love, and they've proven to pretty much everybody's satisfaction they can do it and do it well. Only last year, Cobb and Funk, the youngest of the Mercury 13, went on a trip to see the troops in Korea, and everyone over there seemed happy to have real live astronauts visiting them. The pilots were quizzing Cobb on what it was like in space, how did she fly the spacecraft, they wanted to know everything. And all she could say in reply was, it's the greatest feeling in the world, it's like down here doesn't matter anymore, it's like you want to stay up there *forever*. Of course, she didn't mention spending days in a tiny spacecraft, unable to bend her knees until she thinks her legs will never straighten again, the diapers and catheters and being poked and prodded by doctors before and after every flight, the G4C spacesuit with its six layers of nylon and Nomex which pinch and rub... It was all about the wonder and the going higher, further, faster. Even so, she was never very good with words and has always been a reluctant speaker, and she was uncomfortable with all the attention.

But now she peers out through the tiny window in the hatch at the spy satellite and she wonders what they're doing here and when mission control is going to tell them.

Cobb asks capcom if they're expected to EVA.

At this time no EVA is indicated, capcom replies. Can you confirm the alternate Agena looks to be in good order?

Gorelick in the right-hand seat is nearer to the KH-4B. She lifts the visor on her helmet and leans forward until her nose is only a few inches from the window before her.

It doesn't look damaged, she says, it looks fine.

Cobb is wondering if she's looking at the future of the space programme: will they be no more than orbital repair technicians, rendezvousing with satellites and fixing them in situ? The exercise with the real Agena is all part of the plan to go to the Moon. Next year, the first of the new Apollo spacecraft leaves the North American Aviation factory in San Diego, and though there's one more Gemini flight planned, it's expected Apollo I will launch in early 1969.

But to what end? For what purpose?

DOWN

Though he never said anything, McIntyre was surprised when the kludge worked as intended and scooped up the bucket from the ocean bed. The bucket is not exactly intact—it hit the sea surface pretty goddamned hard, has split down one side, and long snakes of film have escaped from the stacks and now hang down through the bars of the kludge. McIntyre tells Stryker to drop the shot ballast—not all at once, because they don't want to strain the damaged bucket too much or give the kludge an excuse to drop what it carries. And as the Trieste II begins its effortless rise from the ocean bottom, so McIntyre feels his spirits begin to lift, and his mind flies across the miles to the Washington Navy Yard and he knows more than ever he made the right move when he transferred to the Navy Experimental Diving Unit. He's not enjoyed this dive and he feels no real sense of accomplishment at having retrieved the bucket. The Trieste II is too fragile a mistress, and though this descent has gone relatively smoothly—nothing broke!—he remembers all too well others where one damn thing after another went on the fritz. Which is not to say saturation dives are always snafu-free, or that mistakes and malfunctions cannot also prove fatal.

But, he has to admit, spending hours inside a steel ball seven feet in diameter cannot compare with the freedoms of saturation diving, the ability to move about underwater unrestricted, chained only by an umbilical—because at those pressures air in bottles would last mere minutes—limited only by his own physical endurance. True, the Trieste II can take him so much deeper—he's here now on his way back up from 19,500 feet beneath the surface!—while the deepest he's dived on helium-oxygen is 600 feet, and he had to spend six days in a steel can decompressing afterwards.

He looks across the pressure-sphere at the tiny window which gives the only direct view the three men have on the world outside. It's a circle of inky blackness in the curved steel, and his eyes play tricks and he sees it as a pool of infinite depth, an opening without end in the steel, a shaft through the abyss and the hadal zone into who-knows-where and who-knows-what...

Then, nine hours later, as they near the surface and reach the depth at which sunlight can penetrate the water, the black window begins to pale and fade to blue, day dawning on their submarine world, and it glows ethereally like a beacon signalling sanctuary. So McIntyre gets down on his knees and peers through the window, and there's the kludge and trapped in its tines the bucket, and strips of films are hanging out of it like those fronds of rusty growth on the wrecks deep below, but they're fluttering like kelp in the vortices generated by the bathyscaphe's ascent.

At thirty feet, Taylor pays out the cable on the kludge, so when the Trieste II breaches the surface, the bucket will stay thirty-five feet below, where perhaps it will remain intact and not suffer the battering it would receive at the surface. McIntyre, still looking out through the window, sees a column of boiling white turbulence arrow down past the pressure-sphere. The bubbles evaporate to reveal a diver, who gives McIntyre a thumbs-up and then turns to the bucket in the kludge. And as they both watch, a strip of film separates from a film stack and snakes its way downwards, returning to the depths.

Taylor pumps the access tube free of water, and he and McIntyre open the hatch, while Stryker sets about turning off the onboard systems they won't need now they're on the surface. The tube is cold and smells of brine and something infernal, and then the stink generated by three men in a sealed steel sphere overwhelms it. He hears a clanging from above and worms his way into the tube and cranes his neck to look up just as someone opens the hatch and a shaft of clear blue morning sky spears down, causing him to blink and put a hand to his brow. He scrambles upright and clambers up the ladder, and moments later he steps out of the sail onto the bathyscaphe's fairwater decking. He can't help pulling in a deep breath of sea air, and he grins at the USS White Sands rocking on the swell a hundred feet away, and the USS Apache on station beside the auxiliary repair dock, and the boat butting up against the Trieste II's float with a pair of divers hanging from its gunwales.

He wants to say, By God, it's good to be back; but he guesses his face says it for him anyway.

He hears the slap of waves against the bathyscaphe, the bump and scrape of the boat's prow against the fairwater decking, the guttural burble of its idling outboard; and the sunlight bounces from the restless sea surface in fractured sheets of brightness, and there's a depth—it's not the right word but nothing else springs to mind—a *depth* to the colours, to the aquamarine of the water, the scuffed whiteness of the fifteen-foot boat, the implacable grey of the USS White Sands and USS Apache, the ineffable blueness of the sky...

McIntyre stands on the Trieste II, his hand to his brow, he wants a cigarette but that's going to have wait until he's back aboard the USS White Sands, and he feels a bit like one of those Ancient Greeks or Romans who journeyed into the Underworld but escaped back to the surface, only he can't remember the guy's name and he can't remember where he came across the story and he can't really recall the details of it, just something about the woman he went to fetch deciding to stay with her husband...

But he sort of feels like him, anyhow.

Cobb has missed out on the firsts so far, for all that she felt she deserved them. The Mercury 13—though there are only a dozen left in the programme, since Hart retired after her one flight to work directly for the women's movement—was her doing, after all. She was the first American to orbit the Earth, but the Russians did that first; she was the first American to spacewalk, but again after a Russian had done it before her. The only first left, the one not even the Russians can beat, is the first human being to walk on the Moon. That's what the Gemini and Apollo programmes are for, and Cobb is the most senior astronaut in the corps. That is her dream.

Only now they're taking it away from her.

The Korean War is finally over, MacArthur chased the Chinese over the border sixteen years ago, and the war dragged on and on, lasting four times longer than the Second World War, eating up men and materiel, and through it all the USA put thirteen women into space on a regular basis. But now the soldiers are returning home, and Cobb has heard that NASA intends to train men as astronauts and rumour has it some of those will go to the Moon. She's been doing this for seven years, this is her fourth flight into space, and they expect her to step down from the programme and let the men take the lead. She saw this happening more than twenty years ago, after the Second World War, when Rosie the Riveter had to hang up her rivet gun and put her apron back on. Cobb was too young to fly in Cochran's WASP, but when the men came home and women went back into the kitchen, she knew it wasn't for her and became a pilot instead—even though it was hard, really hard, for her to find jobs. Now... Now, she has flown three types of spacecraft, she has even flown supersonic jets, she's not giving this up. God put her here on this Earth for a reason and it is not to "pick up the slack" after the men have had their go.

NASA have already pulled back on their plans. Though they have four years to go, it's clear they're not going to make the president's aim of putting an American on the Moon in time. So Apollo II has been tasked with an orbital rendezvous with a spy satellite in order to perform in situ repairs. That Gemini 10 rendezvous, that was just proof of concept, Irene Leverton and Jan Dietrich did the same in Gemini 11. Cobb had hoped to be given command of Apollo I, but that went to Cagle, Cochran's favourite, it was just a short flight to prove the hardware. Once again Cobb is second, as she has been in everything, and she's commander of Apollo II, with B Steadman as pilot and new recruit Betty Miller as flight engineer. Miller was one of the eighteen who took the Lovelace Clinic tests back in 1961, she failed then but the selection requirements were relaxed given the experiences of the Mercury 13. It's not like Miller is unqualified—she was the first woman to fly solo across the Pacific, from California to Australia, six years ago, she even received the FAA Gold Medal from the president for it. Her lucky troll, Dammit, sat in the simulator during the training for this mission, but it's not up here in orbit in the real spacecraft.

The KH-4B spy satellite is in an orbit with a perigee of 95 miles and an apogee of 240 miles, and has already been boosted once before the atmosphere captured it and caused its orbit to decay. Apollo II's mission is to fix a jammed spool on the intermediate roller assembly, the mechanism which feeds the film from the cameras to the film stacks in the recovery vehicles. Whatever the spy satellite has been photographing, it must be important to go to all this trouble, though now that the Moon is slipping out of reach perhaps Cobb should be grateful Apollo II has reason to be thrown into orbit.

Once they've matched orbits with the satellite, Cobb needs to go EVA. All three are still in their spacesuits, so they attach gloves and helmets and switch the oxygen to the suit circuit. They each verify their helmets and visors are locked and adjusted, their O₂ connectors are locked, and their relief valves open.

SUIT GAS DIVERTER pull to egress, says Miller, reading from the EVA checklist. SUIT CABIN RELIEF – SUIT CIRCUIT RELIEF to close, CABIN GAS RETURN open.

Their suits are at 3.7 psi, they've depressurised the command module, and Steadman pulls down on the handle on the crew access hatch; and in eerie silence, there's only the sound of her own breath in her helmet, Cobb watches the battens withdraw, the hatch pop its seal and swing open to reveal the luminous blue that is the Earth below.

It's beautiful, says Miller.

Help me, B, says Cobb.

She takes the rim of the hatch in either hand and pulls herself up and out and abruptly she's no longer floating horizontally but standing upright, half in and half out of the command module's hatch. The silvery bright cone that is the Apollo spacecraft stretches before her, her ghostly white reflection smeared across it. She turns about and she can see the curve of the Earth, and at the horizon the radiant band of atmosphere which girdles it. She can see clouds drifting across the face of the world and she thinks, I want to do this forever. She remembers her first EVA on Gemini 4 and her reluctance to return to the spacecraft, and she's lost none of the awe she felt then, if anything it now seems even more focused, more spiritual, more affirming.

She pushes herself from the command module and her umbilical slithers out after her. The KH-4B hangs in the sky some thirty feet away, a pale grey cylinder bright with reflected sunlight. It has ejected one recovery vehicle already and the bright gold mylar dome of the second now caps its length. Cobb takes her hand-held manoeuvring unit, her zip gun, and uses it to propel herself across the gap between the two spacecraft. She rolls over and sees one of her crew is now standing in Apollo II's hatch, unidentifiable behind a gold visor.

Is that you, B? Cobb asks.

In the hatch? Yes.

Cobb turns back to face her destination and she raises the zip gun and takes aim at it, and she thinks maybe it's an affront to nature and to God to populate this place with tools which serve a military purpose. The space programme has never been military, for all that it was in a race with the enemy, the USSR; and now finally these ploughshares, these chariots of Apollo, are going to be bent into swords, even as the war below has finally stuttered to a long and drawn-out end.

She's moving too fast, the zip gun isn't powerful enough to check her velocity. She puts up her hands, touches the KH-4B and slides down it, and her umbilical brings her to an abrupt halt and she swings about, banging both feet against the side of the satellite. She hangs there beside it and she knows her heart-rate is elevated, she's feeling warm, the water circulating through her Liquid Cooling Garment isn't cold enough to wick away the heat, and she feels as bent out of shape as the shadow she casts across the KH-4B's curved side. She puts her hands to the spacecraft but there's nothing to hold onto, she bobs at the end of her umbilical and she has no leverage to do anything but hang there. It's a hard scrabble to explore the length of the spy satellite, to move herself around its circumference, and before long she's panting and sweating and her arms are aching, and all the time she's telling mission control what she's doing.

When she does find the right panel, she takes a screwdriver, specially designed to be used with spacesuit gloves, and tries to unscrew the panel's fastenings. It's not working. As soon as she attempts to twist the screwdriver, her legs swing out and she cannot apply any turning force. She considers using the screwdriver as a pick, jamming it through the thin aluminium side of the KH-4B, so it will hold her steady.

Exhausted, she floats away from the spy satellite.

Turning gently about, she finds herself gazing out at an ocean of stars. The KH-4B is forgotten, and she's reminded of the hours she spent in a sensory deprivation tank back when she was paving the way for women to become astronauts, only then she lay in total darkness and absolute silence, she didn't have this sea of light above her, these endless questions and instructions from mission control and B in her headset. She tells them she needs to rest, and her feet and hands are getting cold, but she'll be fine in a minute, and she closes her eyes and relaxes, in her mind's eye she can still see the Milky Way flowing across the sky. She is immersed in Creation, she lets it wash across and over and through her, and she knows this is not something she will ever give up.

Recovered, she fires her zip gun to push her back to the spy satellite. She uses the screwdriver to lever up an edge of a panel, and that becomes a handhold, and a fulcrum, so she can turn the screwdriver. But even that doesn't help, so she reluctantly admits defeat. She puts her booted feet against the spy satellite's side and launches herself back toward the Apollo command module. As she floats past the golden cone capping the KH-4B, she spots motion and, as she watches, the recovery vehicle is ejected and falls away. Fortunately, the KH-4B is pointed away from the Apollo II spacecraft and the bucket arcs away and down a good forty feet from the command module.

Steadman twists to watch it go and says, Was that supposed to happen?

I don't know, says Cobb.

She watches the gold recovery vehicle dwindle and fall to Earth, and she knows it might as well be the Moon that's falling away from them. Even if the rumours are not true about NASA selecting male astronauts, then the Apollo programme is likely to never get any higher than this, to go any further than this. The fighting is done but the war is not over, it will never really be over, and up here is not God's own undiscovered country but just the generals' high ground, it's just the place that has the greatest view, a God-like view.

And Jerrie Cobb, who wants to be the first human being to walk on the Moon, can feel her dreams receding even as the KH-4B Corona recovery vehicle shrinks to a dot against the azure sky and then vanishes.

DOWN

By the time they've lowered the shipping container into the water and the divers have oh-so-carefully transferred the film stacks into it, by the time they get the shipping container aboard the USS White Sands and into the giant refrigerator purposely built to hold everything at the same temperature as the ocean bottom, no one is all that confident there's going to be much left that's salvageable. McIntyre hopes whatever surveillance the spy satellite was doing isn't too important, or maybe they have some other source of intelligence; because to him those film stacks don't look like they're going to be easy to get workable photographs off.

Mooney crosses the deck to McIntyre, who is by the rail enjoying his first cigarette in over twelve hours, and McIntyre's eyes feel gritty from being awake so long and watery from the brightness and blueness—and yeah, maybe a bit from the smoke too—but he's not ready to hit his bunk just yet.

I hear you had a bit of trouble down there, Mooney says.

McIntyre nods. He flicks his cigarette stub out into the Atlantic. I guess, he says. We couldn't get a peep out of dot zero and all those wrecks made it harder than we expected.

There's no wrecks on the charts, Mooney says.

It's 20,000 feet deep, points out McIntyre. How would anyone know?

He shrugs. We found the bucket, he adds. Good luck getting anything useful out of it.

The spooks want a debriefing, John.

Yeah, I guess.

McIntyre looks across at the refrigerator, a white box eight feet by eight feet by eight feet with a cooling unit attached. He's not sure what the spooks want to hear from him, he's not sure what he wants to say to them. They asked him to fetch the bucket; he fetched the bucket. It's not like he should have been here anyway. They only flew him in when the original commander of the Trieste II put himself in hospital; and now it's all over, they'll fly him back to Washington and the Navy Experimental Diving Unit.

He follows Mooney to the superstructure and they step through a hatch and along a gangway and into the ward room. The two spooks are there, sitting at the table, looking as hot and flustered as they had at the briefing. Stryker and Taylor have gone to their bunks, on McIntyre's orders—and he wishes he had gone too. There's no need for this now, it could wait until later.

McIntyre pulls out a chair and sits. You got your film, he tells the spooks, but I don't know how usable it is.

The CIA guy with the spectacles gives a tight smile. Eastman Kodak, he says, assures us the imagery is recoverable.

We took every precaution, the other spook adds. We're confident we'll get to see what we want.

I guess, McIntyre says.

Were there any problems retrieving the bucket? asks one of the spooks.

You mean did everything go to plan, right? McIntyre shrugs. We were lucky not to snag the trail ball on one of the wrecks, he says, and maybe it was a bit harder than anticipated, but no, nothing major went wrong.

I hear you found a lot of shipwrecks.

And airplanes, replies McIntyre.

Anything you saw we should know about? the spook asks.

McIntyre yawns. No, he says, some World War Two airplanes, some freighters about as old, maybe older. Been down there a long time, by the looks of them.

He readies himself to leave, the tiredness has caught up with him and he's trying to decide if he should ask for coffee or just head straight to his cabin.

Anything happen up here I should know about? he asks.

Not much, says the other spook, the one without the glasses. NASA only just went and put a man on the Moon.

CHARM

Once the Trieste II has been emptied of gasoline, floated into the USS White Sands' aft dock well, and the well drained, the USS Apache takes the USS White Sands under tow. The IOU steams south, leaving its station over the Puerto Rico Trench, and heads for Roosevelt Roads. McIntyre is no longer needed, so a utility boat speeds him ahead and he arrives at the naval station hours before the two ships. By the time they dock, he is somewhere over Cuba in a Navy CT-39E Sabreliner jet, soon to rejoin the Navy Experimental Diving Unit, his short time aboard the Trieste II bathyscaphe behind him and safeguarded by orders to never discuss the mission. The refrigerator containing the shipping container of film stacks is transported in a grey USN Dodge M37 cargo truck from the docks to the air station, where it is loaded into a waiting Navy C-130 Hercules. The two CIA men also climb aboard; no one from the IOU joins them.

Forty minutes later, the C-130 rolls down the runway, props buzzsawing, and rises ponderously into the air. The landing-gear folds neatly away, the aircraft banks gently to the right and heads north for Rochester, New York, where the Eastman Kodak film processing centre is ready to recover whatever imagery is possible from the film stacks.

Speed is of the essence as no one is sure what is

happening to the film in the surface-pressure cold water in the shipping container. After all, the bucket has been on the bottom for over a month, where the pressure is four tons per square inch. The C-130 gets a priority slot in the Greater Rochester Airport landing pattern, and as soon as it is on the ground, it taxies towards the military terminal in the south quarter of the field. The rear ramp lowers and the refrigerator is pushed out by the cargo master while the two spooks stand by and watch. An umarked civilian Ford C-600 box truck drives up, followed by a forklift, the refrigerator is loaded into the back of the truck, which leaves the airport, takes Route 47 into Rochester, and then Route 104 into the city centre and the Eastman Kodak film processing plant beside the Genesee River.

Inside the centre, the film stacks are transferred to a refrigerated tank of water prepared weeks before. The remains of the bucket are carefully removed, and the stacks are opened and the film strips examined. Sea water has caused the emulsion gelatin to expand, and this has kept the centre of the rolls of film sealed. Technicians carefully despool the film and those sections of it with recoverable images are dried and then developed. Of the 52,000 feet of film, roughly one tenth has survived and is capable of being processed. The rest is unusable.

The two CIA men oversee the development process, and when the first 8 by 12 photograph slides out of the film processing machine, one of the spooks steps forward and grabs it. He passes it to his colleague, and they both shrug in puzzlement. The photograph appears to show a vast army base outside a city, but neither of them recognise the city or the base. It is certainly not in the US.

The final set of developed photographs and fixed negatives are packed into a secure briefcase. A Ford Galaxie sedan takes the CIA men back to Greater Rochester Airport, where a civilian Bell 205 waits for them on the apron. They clamber into its passenger compartment and buckle themselves onto the bench seat. The pilot turns round and gestures at his headphones. The spooks take the headphones hanging on hooks beside their seats and fit them over their heads.

After one of the spooks has slid the door shut, the helicopter takes to the air and flies south. The CIA headquarters are 293 miles away, a two-hour flight. One of the CIA men clutches the briefcase containing the photographs from the sunken bucket on his lap, the other stares out of the window at the passing countryside. Neither talks, nor pays much attention to the voice of the pilot and various air flight controllers in their headphones.

The heliport at CIA Headquarters, Langley, Virginia, has the FAA code 84VA, it is one hundred feet by one hundred feet. The Bell 205 settles squarely in its centre and before the rotor has even stopped turning, the CIA men have jumped out and are running bowed toward a black Dodge Polara sedan waiting at the edge of the pad. The car takes them to the entrance to the headquarters, where they are met and escorted to a photographic analysis office. There is a palpable air of urgency—before leaving Rochester, one of the spooks called his supervisor and told him what the photographs showed.

It takes a team of analysts only thirty minutes to identify the city in the photographs as Shenyang in northeast China, 100 miles from the North Korean border. According to present intelligence reports, there is only a typical military presence in the city, but the photographs from the spy satellite say otherwise. Worse, at least half of the military vehicles assembled at the base do not display the red star of China but the white star of the USSR. There are Soviet T-64s and BMP-1s and SA-9 Gaskins on BRDM-2s and FROG rockets on their transporter erector launcher trucks, and Chinese Type-63 and Type-69 tanks and what looks like Chinese-badged Soviet troop carriers and trucks, lots of trucks. At a nearby airfield are Soviet Tu-95s and Tu-22s and Tu-16s and MiG-21s and Su-17s, and Chinese H-6s and J-7s. It is a vast Sino-Soviet task force, and it appears poised to enter North Korea. The area has been at peace for over a decade, but this will clearly not remain true for much longer. An invasion of North Korea is worrying, but a military pact between China and the USSR is greater cause for concern.

News of the intelligence unearthed by the sunken bucket from the spy satellite flies up the chain of command. The director calls the president, the joint chiefs of staff are informed. A meeting is arranged in the Pentagon, and another in the White House.

The peace has always been precarious and it seems it is about to be rudely shattered. This cannot be allowed.

Something must be done.

STRANGE

The giant swept-wing Convair B-60 bombers roll along the taxiway at Eielson AFB outside Fairbanks, Alaska. As each one reaches the end of the runway, they halt and wait for permission to take off. The roar from their eight J57-P-3 turbojets is immense, a tsunami of noise that sweeps across the air force base, shaking doors and rattling windows. As each aircraft is given clearance, it begins to trundle forward, huge and seemingly incapable of flight, gathering speed until the great silver shapes slowly unstick from the earth, rising elegantly and effortlessly into the air. The great bogies of their landing gear lift up and into the wings with a series of thunks and whirrs, and the jet bombers power up into the white polar sky, trailing four lines of brown smoke, gradually fading from sight into the limitless distance.

The Convair B-60 has a combat range of 2,920 miles, but it is just over 3,600 miles to the North Korean border with China. The bombers will be met en route by KC-135 Stratotankers out of Clark Air Base in the Philippines for mid-air refueling, both on the flight to China and on the flight home.

Within the 171-foot length of the B-60's fuselage, the crew of ten keep a weather eye open for attacking aircraft. They are in constant contact with Tin City Air Force Station on Seward Peninsula, the most westerly point of land on the North American continent. But they do not know who they should be looking for, Chinese or Soviet. They know only that the massive concentration of forces just north of the Korea border cannot be permitted. The nine megaton B53 nuclear bomb in the bomb bay of each aircraft will see to that.

The US has not been at war since it pulled out of Korea in 1953, and it is not about to see that conflict re-ignited... even if it means using nuclear bombs to prevent it. But the joint chiefs of staff and the president have determined that nothing less will be effective against such a large enemy force.

The B-60s power through the arctic sky, their contrails invisible in the white haze. At an altitude of 53,000 feet, they are above the cumulonimbus cloudbase, and their cruciform shadows run dream-like across the pillowy landscape below. It is peaceful and serene up here, and though the muffled roar of the turbojets is a constant reminder, each crew-member can forget the purpose of their mission, the destruction they have been ordered to wreak, and instead focus on the greater aim, their pursuit of the greater good.

They are peacemakers—and like all effective peacemakers, they are effective because they carry a big stick...

And they are not afraid to use it.

The term "bathyscaphe" was coined by Swiss inventor Auguste Piccard in 1946. After achieving the highest altitude ever reached by a human being in 1938, using a stratospheric balloon, Piccard turned his attention to the depths of the sea. The Trieste was the third bathyscaphe designed by Piccard, and was completed at a shipyard in Trieste—hence the name—in 1953.

It comprised a large float containing a liquid of lighter density than water, typically gasoline, water ballast tanks and two hoppers of steel shot. Beneath this float hung a steel pressure-sphere seven feet in diameter, in which the crew of two travelled. Piccard lived and worked in Belgium, and was Hergé's inspiration for the character of Professor Calculus in his Adventures of Tintin books.

After extensive use in the Mediterranean, in 1958 the Trieste was sold to the US Navy. In January 1960, after fitting a new and stronger pressure-sphere, the Trieste descended 35,767 feet to the deepest known part of the Earth's oceans, Challenger Deep in the Mariana Trench in the Pacific Ocean, a feat not matched until 2012.

After the Challenger Deep dive, the bathyscaphe had its original pressure-sphere put back, was given a new float, and renamed the Trieste II. In June 1963, the bathyscaphe was used to help search for the wreckage of the USS Thresher. The first in a new class of nuclear-powered attack submarines, the USS Thresher had sunk with all hands in 8,400 feet of water off the coast of New England during sea trials. After further modifications, including yet another new float, and a new pressure-sphere rated to 20,000 feet, the Trieste II was used in October 1967 to gather data on the wreck of the USS Scorpion, a nuclear-powered submarine which had sunk in 9,800 feet of water 460 miles south-west of the Azores.

On 1 June 1971, the Trieste II was officially placed in service, having previously been listed as "equipment". She was classified as Deep Submergence Vessel 1, and made part of an Integral Operating Unit with the USS White Sands, an auxiliary repair dock, and the USS Apache, an ocean-going tug.

It was as part of this IOU that the Trieste II was sent in September 1971 to an area of the Pacific Ocean just north of Hawaii.

During the Cold War, both the USA and the USSR

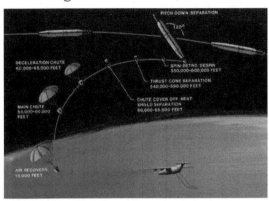

operated a number of spy satellites in orbit. These overflew enemy territory and took photographs of sites of interest to their respective nation's intelligence services. During the 1960s and early 1970s, neither television nor the radio transmission of imagery was at a sufficiently advanced level for this job. As a result, the satellites carried film cameras, and once the film had been fully exposed it was, in US spy satellites, jettisoned and fell to earth in a specially-designed re-entry vehicle, called a "bucket". These safeguarded the film during their fall to earth, much like a space capsule. And, also like a space capsule, the bucket would release a parachute in order to slow its descent. However, rather than splash down into the sea, the bucket would be caught in mid-air by an aircraft fitted with a special hook, typically a USAF JC-130 Hercules flown by the 6549th Test Group out of Hickam Air Force Base on Hawaii.

On 15 June 1971, the latest in the line of Keyhole spy satellites, the KH-9 HEXAGON, was launched from Vandenberg AFB, California. An improvement on earlier KH satellites, it carried four buckets, and 175,601 feet of nine-inch film. Five days after launch, the satellite ejected its first bucket, containing 40,000 feet of film. Due to a damaged parachute, it was not retrieved in mid-air, but allowed to hit the water and sink. Divers then retrieved it. The second bucket, ejected on 1 July, carried 52,000 feet of film and was successfully captured in mid-air. During the recovery of the third bucket, on 10 July, the parachute snapped off and the bucket hit the sea and sank in almost 20,000 feet of water. The final bucket was successfully retrieved by a JC-130 on 16 July.

The retrieved footage was so superior to that produced by previous spy satellites the CIA decided to try and salvage the sunken third bucket. They approached the US Navy, who proposed using the DSV-1 Trieste II bathyscaphe.

The Integral Operating Unit comprising the Trieste II, USS White Sands and USS Apache set out from San Diego on 27 September and headed 60 miles offshore to test the bathyscaphe's ability to retrieve an object from the sea floor. Engineering  corporation Perkin-Elmer had designed and built a "hay hook"—known by the Trieste II's crew as a "kludge"—for the purpose. This fastened on the front of the vessel's float, and was designed to scoop up the film bucket from the ocean bottom. The first dive on 29 September did not go well—several systems aboard suffered electrical problems, and the winch cable jumped the pulley and broke, dropping the hay hook and causing the DSV to ascend 400 feet rapidly. After forty-five minutes of searching, they eventually found both the hook and dummy bucket, but returned to the surface only with the hook.

A second test dive on 5 October also proved unsuccessful when a failure of the navigation computer meant Trieste II could not even locate the dummy bucket. Meanwhile, the US Navy had sent the USNS De Steiguer, a survey ship capable of towing a search fish at depths of more than 20,000 feet, to the search area to find the missing bucket and mark its location with a deep ocean transponder.

On 11 October, during a third test dive, the Trieste II finally located the dummy bucket but lack of time meant they could not use the hook to retrieve it. Confident the hay hook would work as intended, they surfaced. Nine days later, the USNS De Steiguer reported it had found the missing bucket, and had taken photographs of it. The IOU immediately headed for the search zone, arriving on 2 November.

On 3 November, the aft dock well of the USS White  Sands was flooded, the Trieste II was towed out in the Pacific, and the ten-hour-long pre-dive procedure began. This involved loading the float with 67,000 gallons of gasoline and 32 tons of steel shot. Each of the onboard systems was also thoroughly checked out. On 4 November, the USS White Sands headed for a position above the "zero dot", the deep ocean transponder marking the bucket's location, while the Trieste II began her descent. The dive ended at 2 am on 5 November without the bucket being located.

Bad weather then moved in, forcing the IOU to head for Pearl Harbour on 15 November. After a week in port, the USS White Sands, carrying the Trieste II, and the USS

Apache returned to the search zone. Again weather intervened, and the next dive did not take place until 30 November. A leak in one of the shot releases gave the bathyscaphe a 25 degree list to port, making control of the craft difficult. A computer failure also resulted in a loss of navigation data. Despite this, the crew managed to locate the bucket. They were unable to retrieve it but instead planted a deep ocean transponder beside it.

Yet again, bad weather caused a delay. On 5 November, while towing the Trieste II, the bathyscaphe collided with the stern of the USS White Sands, and the towline became entangled with the ship's port station-keeping propeller. While swapping towlines, the Trieste II was sent adrift by a swell, but was fortunately recaptured by the USS Apache. The IOU then returned to port for the Christmas period.

On 25 April 1972, the IOU was back in the search zone, and the Trieste II made its third dive for the sunken bucket. After a 210-minute search, the crew spotted the target. It took six attempts before the Trieste II managed to hook the bucket and lift it from the ocean bottom. Unfortunately, when it impacted the water, the bucket had split, opening the film stacks inside to the sea. As the bathyscaphe rose to the surface, lengths of film up to three feet in length began to break off.

After a nine-hour ascent, the Trieste II reached the surface, and a five-man dive team rushed to reach it. But by the time they arrived, the film stacks had disintegrated, leaving only seven strips of film between three and six feet in length. These were carefully transported to an Eastman Kodak processing plant in Rochester, New York, but the company was unable to salvage any usable imagery from them.

The Trieste II continued in active service with the Pacific Fleet until 1980. In May 1984, she was retired and moved to Submarine Development Group 1. In 1985, Trieste II was moved to the Naval Undersea Museum in Keyport, Washington, where she currently resides.

TOP

On 9 April 1959, NASA introduced seven men to the world. They were the first American astronauts, the Mercury 7: Alan Shepard, Virgil 'Gus' Grissom, John Glenn, Scott Carpenter, Walter M Schirra, L Gordon Cooper and Donald 'Deke' Slayton. NASA wanted to beat the USSR to put a man into space, but the Soviets won when, on 12 April 1961, cosmonaut Yuri Gagarin orbited the Earth. Alan Shepard, the first American into space, made a sub-orbital hop on 5 May aboard the Freedom 7 Mercury spacecraft.

NASA had known for at least two years that the Soviets planned to put a woman into space, but showed no interest in matching the accomplishment, and in fact disingenuously insisted the organisation was not in a "race" with the USSR.

And yet, in late 1959, three separate schemes had set about evaluating women as astronauts.

In August of that year, fifty-eight-year-old pioneer aviatrix Ruth Rowland Nichols underwent centrifuge and weightlessness testing at the Air Research and Development Command at Wright-Patterson Air Force Base, Ohio. Although too old to ever be a serious candidate for astronaut, Nichols was determined to prove she had what it took.

In September 1959 at the annual Air Force Association convention in Miami, Florida, Brigadier General Donald D Flickinger, USAF and Dr W Randolph "Randy" Lovelace II were introduced to a young female pilot called Jerrie Cobb.

Flickinger immediately realised she was an ideal candidate for his Project Woman In Space Earliest, also based at Wright-Patterson.

The third was a publicity stunt, arranged with NASA's full cooperation. During October and November 1959, Betty Skelton, a famous aerobatic pilot and multiple record-holder—on her death in 2011, she still held more combined automobile and aviation records than any other person—  underwent a series of tests by NASA scientists for Look magazine, who published the results in their 2 Feb 1960 issue under the title "Should a Girl Be First in Space?". The article was not a serious attempt at determining Skelton's fitness for the Mercury programme, although she did demonstrate she was a match for the male astronauts.

Unfortunately, when news of Nichols' testing was made public, and she rightly pointed out the medical establishment's lack of knowledge on the workings of the female body, Wright-Patterson Aeromedical Laboratory head Colonel John Paul Stapp (of rocket-sled fame) persuaded ARDC to close down Flickinger's Project WISE. Stapp considered women physiologically and emotionally unable to handle spaceflight: "Economically, the cost of putting a woman into space is prohibitive, and strictly a luxury item we can ill afford." One year later, finding it impossible to find work as a pilot and still dreaming of space flight, Nichols took her own life.

Unable to use the facilities at Wright-Patterson, Flickinger handed over Project WISE to Lovelace. On 14 February 1960, Cobb reported to the Lovelace Clinic in Albuquerque, New Mexico, and underwent the same six days of testing given to the candidates for the Mercury programme. NASA had already declared itself uninterested in Lovelace and Flickinger's research, and so both were careful to explain to Cobb that selection for astronaut training was unlikely to follow completion of the tests. When Cobb passed, and in some tests scored better than the men, they asked her to provide the names of additional women pilots, partly in order to prove her results were not exceptional.

Between 17 January and 15 July 1961, eighteen women pilots were tested at the Lovelace Clinic. Twelve passed. Compare this with the male candidates—thirty-two were tested, eighteen passed (and seven were selected as astronauts). These thirteen women, referred to by Cobb as Fellow Lady Astronaut Trainees (FLATs) but later known as the Mercury 13, were under no illusion the tests they had taken would lead to selection by NASA.

Shortly before the Lovelace Clinic testing took place, Randy Lovelace contacted Jackie Cochran, the most famous and most accomplished woman pilot in the US, who was a close personal friend. Cochran too wanted to be considered for astronaut training, but she was over the age limit and generally not in good health. She was however determined to control any programme involving women astronauts, much as she had done with women pilots during World War II.

In 1942, Nancy Love had persuaded the US Army Air Forces brass to create the Women's Auxiliary Ferrying Squadron while Cochran was in Britain flying for the Air Transport Auxiliary. On learning of this, Cochran was furious—she had made a similar proposal earlier but it had been rejected. She returned to the US and used her many contacts among the USAAF high command to form the Women's Airforce Service Pilots with herself in charge.

Love's WAFS became a part of Cochran's WASP.

In a similar fashion, Cochran would not accept Cobb as the leader of the Mercury 13 and worked tirelessly to take control of the group. While Cobb wanted to prove that she, and by extension the other twelve women pilots, were as capable and qualified as the Mercury 7 and so should be recruited as astronauts, Cochran wanted to create a testing programme to form a pool of suitable candidates should NASA ever decide to fly a woman. This would later prove the programme's undoing.

Once the testing at the Lovelace Clinic had concluded, Lovelace set about arranging for further tests similar to those undertaken by the male astronauts. Because of the incident with Nichols, USAF refused the use of their facilities. Cobb, however, discovered in her home town of Oklahoma City something better than the phase two tests undertaken by the Mercury 7. Psychiatrist Dr Jay T Shurley had built a sensory isolation tank in the basement of the Oklahoma City Veterans' Hospital where he worked. This was far superior to the darkened room used on the male astronauts. Shurley put Cobb in the tank... and she broke all previous records, spending three times as long, in a more isolated condition, than the best of the Mercury 7. The sensory deprivation tank, plus a battery of psychological tests, became phase two of the Mercury 13 programme.

Lovelace managed to persuade the US Naval School for Aviation Medicine at Pensacola, Florida, to lend its facilities for a third phase of testing. In June 1961, Cobb spent ten days at Pensacola, undergoing spaceflight simulation tests in a high-altitude chamber, experiencing the Multi-Place Ditching Trainer and a slow rotation room, and undertaking a variety of physical fitness trials. She passed them all. Arrangements were made for the remaining twelve FLATs to undergo the same regimen of tests, and they were told to report to Pensacola on 18 July 1961—but this was later postponed to 18 September.

Before that could happen, Jackie Cochran, upset because she felt she had been sidelined from leadership of the programme, spoke to Vice Admiral Robert B Pirie, head of US Navy air operations, about her concerns that the Mercury 13 programme was being mismanaged. Pirie wrote to James Webb, NASA Administrator, who responded that NASA had no interest in women astronauts. The US Navy promptly withdrew the use of its Pensacola facilities.

Cobb was still determined to prove she had the "right stuff" and campaigned tirelessly for selection by NASA. She appeared in the press numerous times—her testing at the Lovelace Clinic was the subject of an article in the 29 August 1960 issue of Life, and her time in the sensory deprivation tank also appeared in Life's 24 October 1960 issue. Cochran herself also wrote an article about two of the Mercury 13, twin sisters Marion and Jan Dietrich, which appeared in the 30 April 1961 issue of Parade magazine; and Marion Dietrich penned an article on the testing for McCall's magazine's September 1961 issue.

NASA Administrator James Webb tried to fob off Cobb by offering her a contract as a special consultant for the organisation (however, NASA never asked Cobb to do anything, and she was never paid). But Cobb continued to campaign for NASA to accept some or all of the Mercury 13 as astronauts. If the Russians were planning to put a woman into space, she argued, then here were thirteen opportunities for the US to do it first. NASA was adamant only men could be astronauts, and would not even admit that it had deliberately fixed its entry requirements such that women could not qualify. At that time, such prejudice was not against the law. In 1963, NASA even rejected an African-American astronaut, USAF Captain Edward Dwight

Jr, despite the fact he met all the selection criteria. Cobb continued to campaign for the chance to fly in space, and with the help of Janey Hart, another of the Mercury 13, the wife of a US senator and a seasoned Washington insider, managed to convince Congress to set up a special subcommittee hearing.

Then, on 16 June 1963, Valentina Tereshkova became the first woman in space. This was a blow to Cobb's campaign. Hart was less concerned as she had been pushing an anti-discrimination agenda—the Kennedy administration, after all, had publicly committed itself to gender equality.

For years after Tereshkova's flight, it was rumoured she had performed badly, incapacitated by space sickness and too poorly trained to undertake any useful tasks. In fact, her flight was very successful—much more so than that of Gherman Titov, the second cosmonaut in space. But she too had to deal with discrimination in the USSR.

On 17 July 1963, Cobb and Hart testified before a congressional subcommittee. Although one or two members of the special subcommittee seemed sympathetic, the outcome was a foregone conclusion. When Mercury astronauts John Glenn and Scott Carpenter gave their testimonies, they forcefully insisted there was no need to train women astronauts. "The men go off and fight the wars and fly the airplanes and come back and help design and build and test them. The fact that women are not in this field is a fact of our social order," Glenn testified. That Glenn did not have a degree—one of the qualifications needed to become an astronaut—but was still selected was mentioned but passed over swiftly. Though the Mercury 13 had outperformed the Mercury 7 in many tests, none of the women had flown jets or were jet test pilots, and so "did not meet" NASA selection criteria. The test pilot requirement was dropped later that year—Buzz Aldrin, one of NASA's third intake of astronauts, was never a test pilot. Also not mentioned was Carpenter's poor performance during his space flight, though this omission may have been more to keep confidence in the Mercury programme high.

The biggest blow to Cobb and Hart's campaign, however, came from Jackie Cochran. Since the  Lovelace Clinic tests, Cochran had been insisting she was in charge, writing to various members of the Mercury 13 laying out her ideas and plans. Cochran testified that she saw no good reason to make a woman an astronaut simply because she was a woman. She re-iterated Glenn's argument that women belonged in the home—even though her own career was an exception to that rule—and opined that it was the job of men to lead the way and for the women to follow on and "pick up the slack".

Although scheduled for three days, the congressional hearing closed after two. Cobb and Hart had lost, and the Mercury 13 went their separate ways. Many had lost, or resigned from, their jobs to take part in the programme. Not all managed to pick up the pieces of their lives, but some did continue over the years to keep the dreams of the Mercury 13 alive. Cobb herself left the US to become a supply pilot for a missionary organisation in South America.

It was not until fifteen years later, on 16 January 1978, that the first women were selected by NASA as astronauts, and a further five years when, on 18 June 1983, the first American woman, Dr Sally Ride, went into space. A woman would not command a flight into space until 23 July 1999: Eileen M Collins, on STS-93.

BIBLIOGRAPHY

_Ackmann, Martha: THE MERCURY 13
    (2003, Random House, 0-375-50744-2)
_Bentley, John: THE THRESHER DISASTER
    (1975, New English Library, 0-450-02589-6)
_Berlitz, Charles: THE BERMUDA TRIANGLE
    (1978, Panther Granada, 0-586-04272-5)
_Cameron, James: GHOSTS OF THE ABYSS
    (2003, Walt Disney Pictures)
_Cobb, Jerrie: WOMAN INTO SPACE
    (1963, Prentice-Hall, Inc., No ISBN)
_Cobb, Jerrie: JERRIE COBB, SOLO PILOT
    (1997, Jerrie Cobb Foundation, Inc., 0-9659924-0-3)
_Collins, Michael: CARRYING THE FIRE
    (1974, Cooper Square Press, 978-0-8154-1028-7)
_Day, Dwayne A, John M Logsdon & Brian Latell, eds.: EYE IN THE SKY
    (1998, Smithsonian Institution Press, 1-56098-773-1)
_Dugan, James & Richard Vahan: MEN UNDER WATER
    (1965, Chilton Books, No ISBN)
_Foster, Amy E: INTEGRATING WOMEN INTO THE ASTRONAUT CORPS
    (2011, The John Hopkins University Press, 978-1-4214-0195-9)
_Glenn, John: JOHN GLENN: A MEMOIR
    (1999, Bantam Books, 0-553-11074-8)
_Godwin, Robert: APOLLO 10: THE NASA MISSION REPORTS
    (1999, Apogee Books, 1-896522-51-3)
_Godwin, Robert: FRIENDSHIP 7: THE NASA MISSION REPORTS
    (1999, Apogee Books, 1-896522-60-2)
_Godwin, Robert: GEMINI 7: THE NASA MISSION REPORTS
    (2002, Apogee Books, 1-896522-82-3)
_Godwin, Robert: GEMINI 12: THE NASA MISSION REPORTS
    (2003, Apogee Books, 1-894959-04-3)
_Hellwarth, Ben: SEALAB
    (2012, Simon & Schuster, 978-07432-4745-0)
_Kubatta, Ulrike: SHE SHOULD HAVE GONE TO THE MOON
    (2007, Ulrike Kubatta)
_Kusche, David Lawrence: THE BERMUDA TRIANGLE - SOLVED
    (1978, New English Library, 0-450-03835-1)

_Life: 'A Lady Proves She's Fit For Space Flight'
    (1960, Life, Vol 43 No 10)
_Life: 'Damp Prelude to Space'
    (1960, Life, Vol 43 No 17)
_NASA: PRESS CONFERENCE MERCURY ASTRONAUT TEAM TRANSCRIPT
    (1959, NASA, No ISBN)
_NASA: APOLLO 9 ONBOARD VOICE TRANSCRIPTION
    (1969, NASA, No ISBN)
_Nolen, Stephanie: PROMISED THE MOON
    (2002, Four Walls Eight Windows, 1-56858-275-7)
_Piccard, Jacques & Robert S Dietz: SEVEN MILES DOWN
    (1961, Longmans, No ISBN)
_Polmar, Norman: THE DEATH OF THE USS THRESHER (REVISED EDITION)
    (2004, The Lyons Press, 978-1-59228-392-7)
_Rich, Doris L: JACKIE COCHRAN: PILOT IN THE FASTEST LANE
    (2007, University Press of Florida, 978-0-8130-3506-2)
_Steadman, Bernice Trimble with Jody M Clark: TETHERED MERCURY - A
PILOT'S MEMOIR: THE RIGHT STUFF… BUT THE WRONG SEX
    (2001, Aviation Press, 0-970-90160-7)
_Thompson, Neal: LIGHT THIS CANDLE
    (2004, Crown Publishers, 0-609-61001-5)
_Waltrop, David W: 'An Underwater Space Station Zebra'
    (2012, QUEST: THE HISTORY OF SPACEFLIGHT, Vol 19 No 3)
_Weitekamp, Margaret A: RIGHT STUFF, WRONG SEX
    (2006, The John Hopkins University Press, 0-8018-8394-6)
_Woodmansee, Laura S: WOMEN ASTRONAUTS
    (2002, Apogee Books, 1-896522-87-4)

ONLINE SOURCES

40th Anniversary of the Mercury 7
  history.nasa.gov/40thmerc7/intro.htm
A Space About Books About Space
  spacebookspace.wordpress.com/
Apollo Flight Journal
  history.nasa.gov/afj/
Apollo Operations Handbook
  history.nasa.gov/afj/aohindex.htm
Beyond Apollo
  www.wired.com/wiredscience/beyondapollo
Big Blue Technical Diving News and Events
  bigbluetechnews.wordpress.com/tag/uss-thresher/
Encyclopedia Astronautica
  www.astronautix.com/
Gemini: Bridge to the Moon
  www.nasa.gov/mission_pages/gemini/
Johnson Space Centre History Portal
  www.jsc.nasa.gov/history/index.html
Mercury: America's First Astronauts
  www.nasa.gov/mission_pages/mercury/
Mercury 13 - Women of the Mercury Era
  www.mercury13.com
National Reconnaissance Office (declassified records)
  www.nro.gov/foia/declass/HEXAGON%20Recovery.html
Naval History Blog (US Naval Institute)
  www.navalhistory.org/2012/01/25/trieste-achieves-depth-record
Naval History Magazine, Vol 27 No 1 (online article)
  www.usni.org/magazines/navalhistory/2013-01/navys-deep-ocean-grab
The Space Review
  www.thespacereview.com/article/1720/1
USS Scorpion Search Operations Phase II
  apache67.blogspot.co.uk/
Wikipedia
  en.wikipedia.org

BONUS MATERIAL

GENESIS OF APOLLO, PART THREE

When I first came up with the idea of the Apollo Quartet, the third book had the working title *The Shores of Earth* and was set some 150 years in the future. Since I was determined to use glossaries in interesting ways in each of the four novellas, I planned to have two in the book, each of which would force the reader to re-interpret the actual story. But it was all a bit vague, and setting the story so far in the future stretched the link to the Apollo programme beyond credulity. So I ditched it. And that left me stuck for a story for the third book of my quartet.

Some months before, I'd stumbled across an online article about a recently-declassified mission to retrieve a spy satellite's film bucket from the floor of the Pacific Ocean using the bathyscaphe Trieste II. I've been interested in the Trieste for a couple of years, so I'd made note of the article as a possible idea for a story. But it was not until I mentioned the article to Gavin Smith, author of *Veteran*, *War in Heaven* and *The Age of Scorpio*, that I realised I could use it in the Apollo Quartet. But I needed something else because, of course, the Trieste is not a spacecraft...

At some point, I'd come across mention of Jerrie Cobb and the Mercury 13. I'd initially thought it was while researching women aviators, particularly those of the Air Transport Auxiliary during World War II, for a short story. That story was 'Dancing the Skies' and it was published by exagerratedPress in *The Monster Book for Girls* in 2011. But I recently found an old file dated 2008 which contained notes for a novel partly based on Cobb's career, a sort of alternate history with three alternate timelines—in one, the protagonist becomes NASA's first female astronaut in the early 1960s; in another, the nearest she can get is working as an air hostess; and in the third, she's a pilot for an airline. (I'd used a similar structure back in 2010, but from the point of view of an airline passenger, in 'Travelling by Air', which appeared in the first issue of *Alt Hist* magazine.)

It occurred to me it might be an interesting exercise to imagine a world in which the Mercury 13 became the US's first astronauts. The plot would be simple enough, pretty much a history of the space programme, hitting some of the more notable spaceflights—first American in space, first orbit by an American, perhaps the first rendezvous in orbit by Gemini, the first Apollo mission... But given that I needed to expand the Korean War to explain why NASA selected the Mercury 13, I didn't think going to the Moon would be politically likely in this alternate history. Since I had a spy satellite in the Trieste narrative, why not have the female astronauts service those satellites?

So there was my second narrative thread for Apollo Quartet 3. A quick google for a poem about the god Apollo found me a suitable title in a Homeric hymn, and so the book became *Then Will The Great Ocean Wash Deep Above*.

I'd designed the structures of *Adrift on the Sea of Rains* and *The Eye With Which The Universe Beholds Itself* very deliberately, and I planned to do the same for this third book. The two narratives I planned to write were not, on the face of it, even remotely related. As I'd labelled the sections in *The Eye With Which The Universe Behold Itself* using the year each narrative takes place, I ought to do something similar in this novella—and since one narrative was about space and the other about the bottom of the ocean, "up" and "down" immediately suggested themselves. And that made me think about quarks... Perhaps I could use the different flavours of quarks as section headings?

And from quarks, it wasn't much of a jump to quantum mechanics, and then to the many-worlds interpretation. I thought about presenting several different endings for the reader to choose from, but I still didn't have a link between the two stories. Each took place in entirely separate alternate realities—well, at least one did, but the other could be set in our world. (Having said that, look up the

Convair B-60, mentioned in the section titled 'Strange'.) I did consider not actually linking the narratives, just presenting them as two separate and unrelated stories... But that felt like a cheat. Then one Friday night, as I was walking to the pub to meet up with friends, I realised I could use an *implied* link between the two narratives. What I'd do is have one narrative influence the other— "action at a distance", another link to quantum mechanics. And to show the fragile nature of existence, I'd give the story three different endings. These would take the place of a glossary.

The one thing that was still missing by this point was, for lack of a better term, the Forteana. In *Adrift on the Sea of Rains*, I had the Bell, a Nazi Wunderwaffe; in *The Eye With Which The Universe Beholds Itself*, I'd used the Face on Mars— but I didn't have anything for this story. However, if I moved the Trieste narrative from the Pacific, which is where the real operation took place, to the Atlantic, that not only meant I could use the Puerto Rico Trench as a suitably deep location to require the Trieste, but it also put the action just inside the Bermuda Triangle.

But the more I wrote of *Then Will The Great Ocean Wash Deep Above*, the more I realised I only needed one ending. Instead, I would replace those other two endings with the real world, essays on the inspirations for the two narratives. Initially, I formatted them as appendices, but then I decided I'd not bother but make them part of the story. The abrupt switch from fiction to fact would briefly confuse readers but it would also give both the real world and the alternate worlds more impact.

So, no glossary. And not much in the way of abbreviations either—unlike the previous two novellas. But that didn't matter, even if my original plan had actually centred around the glossaries. Also, this installment would be pure alternate history, with very little in the way of actual science fiction content. But I actually liked that. I'd written *Adrift on the Sea of Rains* to appeal to sf readers of literary fiction, but I'd also written *The Eye With Which The Universe Beholds Itself* to appeal directly to a more science-fictional reader. Doing something different in this novella appealed to me.

Writing *Then Will the Great Ocean Wash Deep Above* proved more difficult than I'd expected because I had to stay true to the real people I was writing about. Fortunately, they were well documented—especially Jerrie Cobb, who was the main protagonist of one of the narratives. She'd written two books, one specifically about her medical testing as the first of the Mercury 13, and I managed to find copies of both on eBay. There were also several books written about the Mercury 13 as a group; and I already had several astronaut biographies I could mine for details on actual space flights.

The Trieste narrative was less of an issue as I had that article about the mission to retrieve a spy satellite film bucket from the floor of the Pacific. But I did have to do some more research about the bathyscaphe, particularly about how the US Navy made use of it—which included tracking down photographs online posted by people who had served aboard USS White Sands, Trieste II's support ship. However, in order to get that narrative started as quickly as possible, I decided to parachute in a viewpoint character. The added benefit of this was that the actual crew of the Trieste II were not very well documented, but by using an invented person that was not an issue. And bringing him up to speed also brought the reader to speed.

So I rejigged American history in order to make an all-female astronaut programme feasible. I needed Jackie Cochran to play an important role, and have political influence, so I needed Eisenhower as president when the programme started as Cochran was good friends with him. This delayed Kennedy's presidency, which meant he couldn't have been assassinated in 1963, and also removed the political will to get to the Moon by the end of the sixties. The latter, at least, worked in my favour.

I took care during the writing of *Then Will The Great Ocean Wash Deep Above* not to mischaracterise the real people I was writing about. Happily, there were enough anecdotes documented so I could use some of them as characterisation—Jerrie Cobb struggling to change from overalls to dress and stockings while approaching Oklahoma City on her record-breaking flight, for example. By relying on such recorded events, I felt I could stay true to the people I was fictionalising. Even then, I had to use some artistic licence—Cobb reveals in her autobiography that she is very religious, and I used that to colour her responses to being in space.

The third book of the Apollo Quartet was, to my mind, the riskiest of the three novellas. I had very little idea how people would respond—it was pure alternate history, the connection between the two narratives was only implied... But the response proved mostly positive. In fact, some people even went on record to say they felt it was the best of the Apollo Quartet so far...

Which does very much increase the pressure on me for book four, *All That Outer Space Allows...*

ABOUT THE AUTHOR

Ian Sales wanted to be an astronaut when he grew up, but sadly wasn't born in the USA or USSR. So he writes about them instead. He also owns a large number of books on the subject. Ian has had fiction published in a number of science fiction and literary magazines and has appeared in the original anthologies *Catastrophia* (PS Publishing), *Vivisepulture* (Anarchy Books), *The Monster Book for Girls* (theExagerratedpress) and *Where Are We Going?* (Eibonvale Press) and *Space—Houston, We Have A Problem* (Ticketyboo Press). In 2012, he edited the anthology *Rocket Science* for Mutation Press. In 2013, he won the BSFA Award for *Adrift on the Sea of Rains* and was nominated for the Sidewise Award for the same work. He reviews books for *Interzone*, and is represented by the John Jarrold Literary Agency. You can find him online at www.iansales.com and on Twitter as @ian_sales.

ACKNOWLEDGEMENTS

My thanks once again to my beta readers, who had a much harder task with this novella than the previous two—Craig Andrews, Eric Brown, Cliff Burns, Stuart Grimshaw, Dave Hutchinson and Jacob Lester; plus additional beta reading by Richard Palmer, Maureen Kincaid Speller and Deborah Walker. Thanks also to Jim Steel for editing duties, Kay Sales for the cover art, and my agent John Jarrold. Because *Then Will The Great Ocean Wash Deep Above* is tied so tightly to real history, writing it proved more of a challenge than I'd expected. This also means it contains a number of real people—in fact, there is only one invented named character in the entire story. I have in all cases tried to be as true as possible to those real people as they have been documented. I apologise if I have failed to do so.

ALSO BY WHIPPLESHIELD BOOKS

The Apollo Quartet, Ian Sales
1 Adrift on the Sea of Rains (2012)
- paperback   £4.99 / $7.50 / €6.00
- ebook: PDF, EPUB, MOBI   £2.99 / $3.99 / €2.99

2 The Eye With Which The Universe Beholds Itself (2012)
- paperback   £4.99 / $7.50 / €6.00
- signed numbered hardback   £6.99 / $12.00 / €8.50
- ebook: PDF, EPUB, MOBI   £2.99 / $3.99 / €2.99

3 Then Will The Great Ocean Wash Deep Above (2013)
- paperback   £4.99 / $6.50 / €6.00
- signed numbered hardback   £6.99 / $10.00 / €8.50
- ebook: PDF, EPUB, MOBI   £2.99 / $3.99 / €2.99

4 All That Outer Space Allows (2015)
- paperback   £7.99 / $7.50 / €7.00
- signed numbered hardback   £9.99 / $11.00 / €9.50
- ebook: PDF, EPUB, MOBI   £2.99 / $3.99 / €2.99

Aphrodite Terra, edited by Ian Sales
- paperback   £5.99 / $8.50 / €7.00
- ebook: PDF, EPUB, MOBI   £2.99 / $3.99 / €2.99

A SNEAK PREVIEW OF

ALL THAT OUTER SPACE ALLOWS

THE FOURTH BOOK OF THE APOLLO QUARTET

Chapter 1
"We choose to go to the Moon"

Ginny is at the table on the patio, in slacks and her favourite plaid shirt, tapping away on her Hermes Baby typewriter, a glass of iced tea to one side, a stack of typescript to the other. Something, a sixth sense, she's developed it during her seven years as an Air Force wife, a *presentiment*, of what she can't say, causes her to glance over at the gate to the yard. And there's Bob, Lieutenant Colonel Robert Lincoln Hollenbeck, cap in hand, his movie-star profile noble with concern. Ginny immediately looks over to her right, across to the Air Force base and the dry lake. Her hand goes to her mouth. Oh my God my God my God. There's a line of dark smoke chalked up the endless sky. My God my God my God. She pushes back her chair and lurches to her feet.

Is it...? she asks.

Have you seen Judy? Bob replies. She's not at home.

Ginny's heart takes wing. *It's not Walden.*

No, she says and she's not thinking straight as she knows Judy is out. She's not at home?

She has to ask: It's Scott?

He ejected in time, Bob explains, but he'll be laid up for a time.

The smoke?

His F-104 hit the ground pretty hard.

Ginny knows the F-104, the one that looks like a silver

missile. With its stubby wings, its sharp-pointed nose and the great burning orifice of its jet-pipe, it could be a starship— no, a *star fighter*... In fact, that's not a bad idea. She pushes her sunglasses up onto her head, picks up a pencil and scribbles a note on a piece of paper.

I think Judy has gone into Lancaster, she tells Bob. She'll be back soon.

I guess I better wait for her, Bob replies. She'll want to go see Scott in the hospital.

Is it bad?

Bob shrugs. Busted leg, he says.

I got some more iced tea in the refrigerator.

He shrugs again and settles his cap back on his head. I guess, he says. He seems to realize he's being unmannerly, and adds, Yes, that would be real fine, Ginny.

Ginny leaves her writing—now is not the time to fill her mind's eye with other worlds and other times. She'll tidy everything away later, once Bob has gone, and before Walden gets home. Walden puts up with it but he doesn't like it, and he especially doesn't like to be reminded of it— his wife, the "space cadette", it was funny, kind of endearing even, back when they were courting at SDSU and afterward, when he was in the Air Force and before she graduated, which she always insisted on doing, and then he proposed. Since their marriage, Walden has used her writing far too many times as a weapon, a club with which to browbeat her into submission when they argue, when he wants his way and their stubbornness is equally matched. He's a liberal guy in many respects and she loves that about him, and perhaps if he had not been Air Force he'd be something wild and crazy; but he's also a man and he runs roughshod over her wishes and desires every moment of every day. She knows only too well which battles she can fight to the bitter end and which are better served by beating a tactical retreat.

But sometimes, too many times maybe, Walden gets his way, and her stories are where she puts the victories she feels she should have won. They're a form of therapy for her, a *catharsis*, a way of vicariously living out a life the real world can't give her, though she wants it so much, was brought up to demand it, remembering with pain and sadness her mother's bitterness as she was marched back into the kitchen when the Second World War ended, "Rosie the Riveter go back home" tattooed on her heart, written in the lines of her face.

Ginny fetches the jug of iced tea and a pair of fresh glasses, and she and Bob settle down in the lounge, on sofas across from one another, the coffee table between them. Sprawled on its top are half a dozen magazines, the cover of the uppermost depicting a beautiful woman in a bubble helmet exiting a spaceship on an alien world, the name "Alice Eleanor Jones" prominent as the issue's novella is hers—but then she's a big name author and has been for the past ten years. Ginny only wishes she were as good as Jones (and she's jealous of Jones's success in the slicks), but she needs to clear the magazines away before Walden gets home. Bob takes his glass, balances it on one knee, his cap now hung on the other knee. Ginny lifts her sunglasses from her crown, bends forward to put them on the coffee table, and uses the movement as an excuse to scoot the magazines together into a pile and then place the pile on the carpet under the table. There's a thin dusting of sand on the table-top and a series of smeared rectangles where the magazines sat—she never moves anything here in the desert, fine sand gathers on every surface—so she gives it a swipe with the flat of her hand before sitting back.

For a minute or so, they smile uncomfortably at one another. Ginny likes Bob, he's a swell guy, but they both know this moment is awkward; and she's wondering what possessed her to invite him in to wait for Judy. He would have been happy sitting in his car, it's not like he can do small talk with a woman, even a "free spirit" like Ginny—that's how Ginny likes to think the guys on the base think of her. (She knows it's probably not true and Walden will tell her nothing; and she tries so much to fit in, even with the other wives but sometimes it's hard and she says something and everyone turns to look at her like she just sprouted a second head.)

This is nice tea, says Bob. Not too sweet.

It keeps me going during the day, Ginny says.

You said Judy went into Lancaster?

Bob takes another sip of his tea, and then glances at his wristwatch.

Ginny looks at her own watch. I'm pretty sure it was about three hours ago, she says. I guess she'll be back any time soon.

Bob rises to his feet. I ought to go wait outside, he says, so I don't miss her.

You'll hear her drive up from here, Ginny tells him.

The room is as silent as the desert, Ginny won't have distractions like the radio playing when she's writing. Her typewritten words drop into the quiet like supersonic jet fighters stooping from the sky.

She thinks, was I being forward? Was that forward? I don't want him to read too much into that, maybe I'm being too relaxed. It's only Bob, but... She sits up straight, prim and proper, despite the slacks and shirt, despite the strappy slingback sandals and the chipped polish all too visible on her toenails, and says, But if you think that's best...

Bob nods. I think so, he says.

His face is a mask, but Ginny thinks maybe she detects some relief. And she wonders if maybe spending the morning in the head of her story's heroine is making her see things in that handsome countenance which don't exist, her imagination spilling over into the real world and laying a deceptive gloss over it. It's okay when she's with Walden, she knows him so well, she can read him like, well, like *a book*. And when there's company over, she's usually had all day to prepare for it, to rehearse for the role she must play, dashing from room to room getting them clean and tidy, getting the food ready, getting everything *just right* like she's supposed to...

Bob puts his cap on his head and carefully straightens it. It was nice tea, he says, Thank you, Ginny.

So she rises to her feet, and says, You're coming on Sunday, aren't you? To the barbecue?

Sure, he replies, Alison and I are looking forward to it. He gives a curt nod. You'll tell Wal I was here, he says (and it's clear from his tone it's not a question).

Of course, Ginny tells him.

She sees him to the door, the front door this time, not the French windows onto the patio, and she watches as he crosses the road and climbs into his blue sedan. There's a cough and a dyspeptic rumble as he starts the engine, but the car remains in place, engine idling, occupant gazing fixedly forward.

Ginny closes the door slowly and returns to the lounge. She tidies away the iced tea, rinsing the glasses, drying them and putting them in a cupboard, returning the jug to the refrigerator. It's getting close to five o'clock and Walden will be home just after six, so she heads out onto the patio to pack up her typewriter and manuscript. She sees the note she scribbled earlier and gazes down at it; and then thinks, Oh my, you silly. F-104. She knows about them, Walden has flown over a hundred hours in F-104s. It's the Lockheed F-104 *Starfighter*. She knows that, why would she write something as silly as "like a star fighter". It was Bob, his appearance threw her.

Ginny gathers up her typescript into a buff folder, and carries it and the Hermes Baby inside. After she has put away her writing things, and the magazines from the lounge, she makes herself ready for Walden. She brushes her hair, puts on lipstick and powder, checks her appearance will pass inspection, and goes to make dinner. It's all part of the job of being an Air Force wife, presenting a normal home-life so her husband can briefly forget how close he comes to "buying the farm" each day. It's a small price to pay, she loves Walden, her love remains undiminished from the day they wed—although that doesn't mean they haven't argued, they haven't spent days refusing to talk to each other. Ginny's mother brought her up to be independent, to have expectations, ambitions and, okay, marrying an Air Force pilot wasn't the smartest move she could have made in that regard—

Unlike many of her friends, Ginny didn't go to university to catch herself a husband, she stayed and matriculated, married Walden a month after she received her Lit degree. She never used her BA, of course, she joined her husband in the United States Air Force. But she has her stories, she has her imagination, and because Walden allows her that she's willing to play the dutiful Air Force wife for him.

At six thirty, she hears a car pulling up, and then the tigerish roar it makes as it slides into the carport and the engine-noise bounces off the walls. She smiles, her flyboy is home.

He strides into the kitchen minutes later, where she's stirring gravy, puts his arms about her waist, sticks his nose into her hair, breathes in deeply and then plants a kiss on the top of her head.

You hear about Scott? he says.

Bob was here, looking for Judy, she replies.

Damn bad luck. He's going to be grounded for months with that leg.

And that's all Walden says on the matter.

Ginny exits the house carrying a tray on which sits a platter of raw steaks. The guys are standing about the barbecue— Scott in a chair to one side, busted leg held out stiffly before him in a cast. Walden is making some point emphatically with jabs of a pair of meat tongs. She stops a moment and watches them, watches *him*, her husband, wreathed in a cloak of grey smoke, her flyboy, in his white T-shirt and tan chinos, aviator sunglasses, that wholesome white-toothed smile. And she thinks, so strange that his parents should name him after a book subtitled "Life in the Woods"...

They didn't, of course; I did, I named him Walden for Henry David Thoreau's 1854 polemic. There is a scene in Douglas Sirk's 1955 movie *All That Heaven Allows*—the title of this novel is not a coincidence; the movie is a favourite, and, in broad stroke, both *All That Heaven Allows* and *All That Outer Space Allows* tell similar stories: an unconventional woman who attempts to breaks free of conventional life... There is a scene in the movie in which Ron has invited Cary back to his place for a party. While he and his best friend, Mick, fetch wine from the cellar, Cary is at a loose end and idly picks up a copy of Thoreau's *Walden* lying on a nearby table. She opens the book at random and reads out a line: "If a man does not keep pace with his companions, perhaps it is because he hears a different drummer. Let him step to the music which he hears, however measured or far away." Not only is *Walden* Ron's favourite book, she is told, but he also *lives* it—

Walden Jefferson Eckhardt, however, sees nothing inconsistent between his admiration for Thoreau's book and his career in the United States Air Force. He is a test pilot; and they see themselves as a breed apart, at the top of the pyramid, men of independence and daring and achievement. Walden stands there with his fellow test pilots—and Ginny knows them all—and though they're tall and stocky, blond-haired and brunet, craggy-featured and smooth-faced, they all look the same. Cut from the same cloth, stamped from the same mould.

She starts forward, her heels tock-tock-tock on the patio, because for this gathering she's playing the dutiful Air Force wife and has dressed accordingly. She approaches the men at the barbecue bearing bloody meat for them to char and broil, and they turn carnivorous grins on her, teeth bright through the smoke, eyes invisible behind aviator shades.

Hey, Ginny, let me take that, says Al, reaching out with

both hands for the tray, the neck of a beer bottle clutched between two fingers.

She hands him the steaks, then turns to Walden. Chicken next? she asks.

He has interrupted his anecdote because it's not for her ears. Sure, hon, he says off-handedly.

FEBRUARY, 1968   **Galaxy**   VOL. 26, NO. 3

MAGAZINE

CONTENTS

She's tempted to ask him what he was talking about, but she's uncomfortable under the mirrored eyeless gazes of the guys, so she gives a faint smile and tock-tock-tocks away.

The women are sitting about the table at which Ginny likes to write, nursing drinks, their faces powdered and lipsticked, some wearing sunglasses, a couple with fresh hairdos. And it occurs to Ginny there are more stories at that table than there are when she has her Hermes Baby upon it—and they are *real* stories, not the science fiction she writes, which are set in worlds constructed from, and inhabited by, figments of the imagination; nor are they the stories which appear in *Redbook* or *McCall's* or *Good Housekeeping*, what Betty Friedan calls stories of "happy housewife heroines"—and it's those very stories which drove Ginny, and no doubt many women like her, to science fiction and its invented worlds. Ginny dislikes words such as "prosaic" and "quotidian" because she believes what she writes employs a dimension beyond that, she believes her stories use science fiction to comment on the prosaic and quotidian *without* partaking of it.

But right now the prosaic and quotidian is signalled by a sky like a glass dish hot from the oven and the phatic chatter of four women in bright dresses, the most colour this yard of sparse grass, and its trio of threadbare cottonwoods, has seen for weeks.

Pam looks up as Ginny approaches, leans forward and then slides a martini slowly across the table-top. This one's for you, she tells Ginny.

I still have the chicken to bring out, Ginny replies.

Later, Pam says with a smile. Drink first.

Alison and Connie add their voices, so Ginny takes the free chair at the table and it's a relief to stop for a moment. She lifts the drink and toasts the other women.

These barbecues are a regular occurrence, though they each take it in turn to play host. Here in the Mojave Desert, the days are bright and hot and blue-skied, endless days of dust and heat, and so they lead summer lives throughout the year. Ginny sips her martini and lets the chatter of Judy, Alison, Connie and Pam, and in the background the boasting of the men, wash over her. She has maybe fifteen minutes before the steaks are ready and Walden starts demanding the chicken; because when he wants something he expects to get it, she's here to cater to him after all. Perhaps in private she can make her own demands, set her own limits, but he brooks no dissent on occasions such as this. She takes another sip of her martini and tells herself her "feminine mystique" is for her husband's eyes and ears only—

Ginny's attention is snagged by the rasp of a lighter, and she looks up to see Judy put the flame to a cigarette in her mouth. So Ginny leans forward and asks how she is coping with her invalided husband. In response, Judy sucks in theatrically, eyebrows raised and lips pursed, and then expels smoke in a long plume over the table. The others laugh. It is all too easy to sympathise, they are Air Force wives. Ginny abruptly remembers days in Germany, when Walden flew F-86D Sabre jets for the 514th Fighter-Interceptor Squadron at Ramstein AFB. For all her open-mindedness, her hankering for new horizons, Ginny found Germany a difficult place in which to live, the contrast between life on the base and life outside, life in the US and life in Europe, too stark, too marked for comfort. She was prolific during those two years, her writing helped her cope.

Walden calls out: Hey, hon, chicken!

No rest for the wicked, says Alison.

Ginny gives an exaggerated sigh, drains the last of her martini and then plucks the olive out of the glass. She pops it into her mouth before rising to her feet.

Later, everyone has repaired to the lounge and the radio is playing quietly in the background. Ginny is sitting on the floor at Walden's feet when he throws a newspaper down onto the coffee-table and says to the other guys, Have you seen this?

Bob leans forward and picks up the newspaper, that day's *Los Angeles Times*.

What am I looking at? Bob asks.

NASA wants more astronauts, Walden tells him.

Bob looks down at the front page and reads out: "NASA is looking for men. You must be a United States citizen, not over 36 years old, less than 6 feet tall, with a college degree in Math or Science and with at least 1,000 hours flying time. If you meet all the requirements, then please apply."

Seriously? asks Bob. You thinking of putting your name in?

Yeah, replies Walden. They've put, what, a dozen guys up so far? And the Soviets have launched about ten. They're top of the pyramid now, Bob.

You been keeping track? asks Al (but his grin is a little too knowing).

Ginny is as surprised as the guys, she didn't know Walden was interested in space. Walden has asked about the X-15 program, she knows that; but he has not been assigned to it.

She hopes her husband applies to NASA, and she hopes he is successful. She likes the idea of being married to an astronaut, certainly what she knows of space exploration she finds fascinating and she'd welcome knowing what it's *really* like. Ginny reads and writes science fiction, stories about spaceships and alien worlds, but they're made-up, invented. The Mercury program, the Gemini space capsule—they're real, men have used them to orbit the Earth. They're *actual* in a way Ginny's stories can never be.

The other wives at Edwards, and their husbands, they don't know about Ginny's writing. She hides away the magazines when she has visitors—female visitors, of course; the men simply don't see them, much as they don't see anything they consider of interest only to women—and she uses her maiden name as a byline, because she started sending letters to the magazines as a teenager and became known under that name. Ginny keeps her science fiction life separate and secret from her life as an Air Force wife, it's easier that way. But for all she knows there may well be other subscribers to *Galaxy* and *If* and *Worlds of Tomorrow* at Edwards Air Force Base.

Of course, life here is all about the menfolk, supporting them, providing a stable home life to succour them when they're not risking their lives. Perhaps that's why NASA insists on test pilots—or, at the very least, jet fighter pilots. Because their wives are trained to provide the stability the astronauts need in order to risk their lives so publicly in such an untried endeavour...

If so, then the joke is on NASA: test pilot marriages fracture before test pilot nerves.

—☽—

Chapter 2
T-Minus

Walden says nothing about the physical at Brooks AFB or, months later, the interviews at the Rice Hotel in Houston; but for a week after his last trip to Texas he swaggers more than usual. Ginny knows this unshakeable confidence is as much a coping mechanism as will be, should he fail, his subsequent realisation he doesn't really want it anyway. But she hopes he succeeds, she wishes she could go into space herself, she wishes she could be an astronaut. But she knows that, at this time, it's an occupation reserved for men—no, more than that: reserved for men of Walden's particular stripe, jet fighter pilots and test pilots. She calls him "my spaceman" one night, it just slips out—she is reading the latest issue of *If*, there's a good novelette in it by Miriam Allen deFord, and Ginny's head is full of spaceships and spaceship captains; but Walden turns suddenly cold and gives her his thousand-yard stare. He starts to explain the competition is fierce, he won't know how he's done until he hears from NASA... but he breaks off, scrambles out of bed and stalks from room.

Ginny puts the magazine on the bedside table, but her hand is shaking. She sits silently in the bed, her hands in her lap, and waits. He does not return. Fifteen minutes later and he's still not back, so she rearranges her pillows, makes herself comfortable beneath the sheets, and reaches out and turns off the bedside lamp. She has no idea what time it is when he eventually slides into bed beside her, waking her, and whispers, Sorry, hon. She rolls over, closes her eyes and tries to re-enter the vale of sleep, where marriages are blissful, life itself is blissful, and she is as famous as

Catherine Moore or Leigh Brackett.

They wake at 0500, the shrill ring of the alarm dragging them from sleep. While Walden goes for a shower, she wraps herself in a housecoat and heads for the kitchen. There is breakfast to prepare—coffee to roast, bread to toast, eggs to fry, bacon, beans and hash browns. She does this every day, sees off her man with a full stomach and a steady heart. Here he is now, crisp and freshly-laundered in his tan uniform, hungry for the day ahead. He takes his seat, she pours him juice and coffee, slides his plate before him, and then sits across the table and watches him eat as she sips from a cup of coffee. She should be getting up before him, making herself ready, dressed and made-up, to greet him when he awakes—but countless past arguments have won her the right to make his breakfast and see him off to work without having to do so. The housecoat is enough.

They kiss goodbye at the door, and he strides off to the Chevrolet Impala Coupe in the carport. Though she wants to go back to bed, there is too much to do, there is always too much to do.

After clearing up the breakfast things, she makes herself another coffee and settles down to catch up with her magazines, she is a couple of issues behind with *Fantastic*, and this issue, the last of 1965, features a novella by Zenna Henderson and stories by Doris Pitkin Buck, Kate Wilhelm and Josephine Saxton.

Later, she will get dressed—and she will dress for comfort, not for appearance's sake—and she will get out the Hermes Baby and she will work on her latest story. She made the decision years before to incorporate elements of her own life—and, suitably disguised, Walden's—into her science fiction, so she feels no need to visit libraries or book stores for research. She has a stack of issues of *Fantastic Universe*, *If*, *Amazing Stories*, *Galaxy*, *World of Tomorrow* in a closet—they are all the research material she needs. *Galaxy*, for example, runs a science column by astronomer Cecelia

Payne-Gaposchkin; *Amazing Stories* has featured science columns by June Lurie and Faye Beslow since the 1940s. Walden, of course, has a stack of aeronautics and

---

"The only women in the group beside myself were Virginia Kidd and Donald Wollheim's wife Elsie, who wrote a little and was nominally called a Futurian."

p44, *Better to Have Loved*, Judith Merril

"Gernsback claims he had as many female readers as male, but far fewer women became actively involved with fandom than men. Despite their numbers, the main route to fandom—having your letters published—was blocked to them, perhaps, as Gernsback implies, because they were less interested in engaging with the science of science fiction than men."

p25, *The Battle of the Sexes in Science Fiction*, Justine Larbalestier

"Not only was the female viewpoint unappreciated in most of the '20s, '30s and '40s, but also women were generally relegated to the position of "things", window dressing, or forced to assume attitudes in the corner, out of the way."

p281, *Science Fiction Today and Tomorrow*, Reginald Bretnor, ed.
,'Hitch Your Dragon to a Star: Romance and Glamour in Science Fiction', Anne McCaffrey

"What sort of person writes science fiction? He—it is "she" once in about fifty times—very seldom depends wholly on the writing of science fiction for his living."

p51, *New Maps of Hell*, Kingsley Amis

"A few women, such as C. L. Moore and Leigh Brackett, were working in the field earlier; Katherine MacLean entered the fray in 1949 in *Astounding*."

p258, *Trillion Year Spree*, Brian W Aldiss

"But at the same time [science fiction] has always reflected and continues to reflect a particular type of authority, that of men over women."

p87, *In the Chinks of the World Machine*, Sarah Lefanu

---

engineering texts in the bedroom he uses as a den, and Ginny has on occasion paged through them—not that Walden knows; his den is for him alone and she allows him the illusion of its sanctity; naturally, it never occurs to him to wonder how the room remains clean.

Ginny is feeling lazy today. She likes to think she has an excellent work ethic when it comes to her writing, but some days she finds it hard to muster the enthusiasm to bang on the keys of her typewriter. Especially when she has just read something she thinks she can never approach in quality—and that, she sadly realises, is true of the Saxton story in the magazine she is holding. Josephine Saxton is a new writer, from England, and this is her debut in print. Ginny only wishes her first published story, just four years ago in *Fantastic Universe*, had been as good.

The blow to her confidence decides her: she will leave her current work in progress until tomorrow; today she will catch up on her correspondence, she owes letters to Ursula, Judith and Doris, and she really ought to fire off a missive to Cele at *Fantastic* with her thoughts on the issue she has just read...

After she has showered and dressed in slacks and shirt, she finds herself outside on the patio, gazing east across the roofs of Wherry Housing at the Air Force Base and Rogers Dry Lake, and beyond it the high desert stretching to the horizon, where the Calico Mountains dance in the pastel haze of distance. As she watches, a jet fighter powers up from one of the runways and though it is more than a mile and a half from her, she can tell from its delta wing it is a F-102 or F-106. Its throaty roar crowds the cloisonné sky, there's a quick flash of mirror-bright aluminum as the aircraft banks, and then the fighter seems to fade from view as it flies away from her. She wonders if it is Walden in the cockpit, she has no idea what he does from day to day once he enters the base; officially, he is a research test pilot in the Fighter Test Group, but she does not know what he researches, which fighters he test pilots. Not the North American X-15, she knows that much, an aircraft which intrigues her because it is also a spaceship—it has flown more than fifty miles above the Earth, right at the edge of space, at more than 4,000 miles per hour. And it even *looks* like a spaceship, like a rocket, as much at home in vacuum as it is in atmosphere. She would like to know more about the X-15 but it is a sensitive subject in the house. Walden has tried to get on the program but has been refused, and he wears the refusal badly. Perhaps that's why he was so keen to apply to become an astronaut.

Ginny is a California girl, a *real* one, born and bred in San Diego in Southern California, not one of those "dolls by a palm tree in the sand" from that song on the radio. She has history in this landscape of deserts and canyons and mesas, though she is more used to a land beside the limitless plain of the Pacific. Here in the Mojave she is hemmed in by mountains, they encircle her world, her flat and arid world, where the small towns are so far apart they might as well belong to their own individual Earths. Standing here, gazing in the direction of Arizona, she finds it easy to believe Edwards is the only human place in the world, a lonely oasis of civilisation—and she knows her husband thinks of it as a technological oasis in a world held back from the best science and engineering can offer by the short-sightedness of others. To some degree, she thinks he may be right. But she is also a housewife, and she lives in a world in which beds must be changed, clothes laundered, meals cooked and checkbooks balanced. She envies Walden his freedom to ignore all that—he can have his "life in the woods", but only because she manages his world.

And now she really must get on with her letter-writing... although the lawn looks like it needs mowing and the end of the yard is beginning to look a little untidy...

On Fridays, Ginny drives into Lancaster to do the weekly shopping, there's a commissary on the base but its stock is better-suited to bachelors. Ginny and Walden only have the one car, of course, the Impala, so she accompanies him onto the base and then drives the car back home. He won't let her drive him to work, he has to be behind the wheel, though she's a perfectly good driver, not that he will ever admit it.

Since Ginny has to make Walden's breakfast and be ready to leave when he does, she wakes earlier than him in order to get showered, dressed and made-up. She slides out of bed, leaving Walden breathing as though sleep were an endless sequence of underwater dives, and pads across the bedroom to the bathroom. She showers, she washes her hair, she checks her legs and underarms to see if they need shaving, she pats herself dry and wraps her hair in a towel. In the second bedroom—which is her room in much the same way the third bedroom is Walden's den—her two bookcases holding science fiction massmarket paperbacks and a few hardcovers. Not that Walden sees those books, he thinks the room contains only clothes and cosmetics and shoes (her wardrobe is not as big as Walden believes it is)— and her closet is filled with back-issues of science fiction magazines; but no desk, only a dressing-table with a triptych of mirrors on its top. She sits before this latter piece of furniture and minutely inspects her face...

By the time Walden appears in the kitchen, washed and uniformed, she is dressed in a lemon-yellow short-sleeved A-line summer dress, bought in San Diego during her last visit and not made from a pattern as the other wives would have done (although Ginny is not, perversely, jealous of their facility with sewing machine, needle and thread), face powdered, mascaraed and lipsticked, and her purse waiting on the table in the hall. She dishes out Walden's breakfast and watches him eat it while she sips a coffee. She does not need to glance at her watch to know if they are on schedule—Walden is military, his life is ruled by schedule; he entered the kitchen at the same time he does every weekday, he takes as long to eat his eggs, bacon, hash browns and beans as he always does, he pushes back his chair, drains the last of his coffee, and says, Time to go, hon—right on schedule.

And because it is Friday, she replies, yes, dear. And she rises to her feet, puts his plate and cup, and her own cup, in the sink to be washed later, follows him into the hallway, where she slides on her sunglasses, picks up her purse, and tock-tock-tocks out of the house and into the carport, and waits deferentially while Walden locks up behind her. Once he has slid behind the steering-wheel, she joins him in the car and sits there waiting compliantly as he gives the ignition key a quick, confident twist.

It's the first day of April, the temperature is around 70° F and the sun beats down on the blacktop, causing it to shimmer and flex ahead of her as Ginny drives the thirty miles to Lancaster, her nyloned foot heavy on the throttle, she has shucked her heels as it's more comfortable when driving. Tucked away somewhere in her purse is a shopping list of groceries, but as well as the Alpha Beta Market she also needs to visit Sears to buy herself some more clothes. She and Walden argued last night—he came home angry after some incident on the flight line, he wouldn't say what. She had spent the day writing, he demanded to know why she must dress like a hippy, which only demonstrated to her he has no idea what a hippy looks like, but the remark sparked a row... And now she must, as she has reluctantly promised, dress more often like the other wives in skirts and dresses. She is already thinking how she might use the incident in a story, perhaps something about how wives disguise their true nature by presenting themselves according to their menfolk's wishes and expectations, using all the tools at their disposal: makeup, foundation garments, skirts and heels and the like; maybe, she thinks, the wives could be alien creatures, forced into their wifely roles in order to survive...

There are certainly days when Ginny feels like an alien creature—or rather, days when she feels she has more in common temperamentally with some invented alien being than she does her husband of seven years. Walden is not a complicated man, but there are times when she cannot understand what is going through his head. She knows some of it is a result of a peculiar kind of blindness—he pretends not see her science fiction, and has done for so long now he probably can't *actually* see it. His mind filters out anything that is not of his masculine world. If Ginny leaves out a magazine, a copy of *Redbook*, perhaps, or *Ladies Home Journal*, brought round by one of the other wives, Walden says nothing but behaves as if it exists in a blind spot in his vision. When Ginny leaves pantyhose to dry in the bathroom, he complains of her "mess" but cannot say what the mess is. And should Ginny lose something, a lipstick, an earring, he will happily look for it but he will never find it, she has to do that herself, and she often finds it in a place where Walden has already searched.

She twists the steering-wheel and directs the Impala into the Alpha Beta Market's parking lot, causing it to wallow queasily as it bounces over edge of the road. She finds a parking space quickly and slots the car into it. After sliding her feet into her shoes, she exits the car; and, as she leans in to pick up her purse, she hears her name called. Surprised, she turns about and there's a figure across the lot waving at her. It's another woman, another wife, blonde hair, sky blue A-line summer dress, tanned arms—and it's a moment before Ginny recognises Mary, wife of Captain Joe H Engle, whom she doesn't know all that well as Mary's husband is a pilot on the X-15 program and Walden is still sensitive on that topic; although the four of them have spoken on occasion in the Officers Club on the base, so if not friends then certainly acquaintances.

The two women meet up at the entrance to the supermarket and it's clear Mary has something she wants to talk about, although it's not easy to read her expression due to the large sunglasses she is wearing.

Joe tells me, she says earnestly, that Wal is doing the tests to be an astronaut?

He is, Ginny confirms. Joe too?

They walk into the store side by side.

You think Wal has a chance? asks Mary.

He thinks so, Ginny says.

When do you think they'll be told?

Ginny pulls a trolley from the line and drops her handbag into it. I don't know, she says. Soon, I hope. I'm not sure I can put up with Walden like this for much longer.

She smiles to take the sting from her words, but the memory of the row with Walden is still sharp.

Oh I know, says Mary. Joe's the same, he's not good with all the waiting, you'd think he'd be used to that being a test pilot.

Joe already has an astronaut pin, hasn't he? Flying the X-15?

The what? Oh I don't know, I guess.

Mary pushes her trolley alongside Ginny's and the two make their way along the aisle in formation. As they pick items from the shelves, they discuss what selection by NASA might mean, both for their husbands and for themselves. It's something Ginny, whose interest lies in the launch vehicles and spacecraft, the science and engineering, has not considered. She has a book, hidden in her underwear drawer where Walden will never find it, she has been reading: *Americans into Orbit* by Gene Gurney, "The Story of Project Mercury". One day, she hopes, Walden will be in such a book. But the issues raised by Mary are ones that have not occurred to Ginny: moving to Houston, finding somewhere to live, being in the public eye, interviews in *Life* magazine and on television... She wonders if she wants that—not that she will have any say in the matter if Walden is selected.

If they ask him, he *will* accept—and nothing she can say will prevent him.

The telephone rings but before Ginny can get to her feet, Walden is up and striding into the hallway. She hears him answer, and then it is a succession of yes sir, of course sir, I would be honoured sir, yes sir, I'll be there sir, *yes sir*. Someone from the base, she decides; and returns to her book. Moments later, Walden marches into the lounge and he is grinning fit to break his jaw.

That, he says, was Deke Slayton.

Ginny recognises the name. He is one of the Mercury Seven, although he never flew since he was diagnosed with a heart murmur. She remembers his headshot from page 89 of *Americans into Orbit*.

From astronaut selection at NASA, Walden adds.

She doesn't need to ask, she can tell from Walden's expression.

I report in four weeks, he tells her.

You're going to be an astronaut, she says; and she doesn't quite believe it. She puts down her book. An *astronaut*, she says again in wonder.

He crosses to her, bends forward, grips her about the upper arms and hauls to her feet. I am! he crows. I'm going into space!

He wraps her in a tight hug and she can feel the righteousness beating off him like waves of manly heat. She can also feel where his fingers wrapped her arms and pressed hard enough to bruise.

You might even go to the Moon, she says.

She can't help it, she's grinning too now, she is as excited as he is.

Shit, yeah! The Moon! I'm going to the goddamn Moon!

He whirls her around, and she laughs giddily. Then he pulls her in close again and he says, I wanted this, Ginny, I really wanted it, I wanted it so bad.

You deserve it, Walden, she tells him, you're the best.

She pecks him on the cheek—because she's happy for him, *more* than happy for him, his joy is hers too; and because she loves him.

Later, she knows he will want more.

NEWS RELEASE

NATIONAL AERONAUTICS AND SPACE ADMINISTRATION

MANNED SPACECRAFT CENTER — Houston 1, Texas

HU 3-5111

MSC 66-22
April 4, 1966

HOUSTON, TEXAS Nineteen pilots will join the astronaut team early in May, the National Aeronautics and Space Administration announced today.

They will boost the total number of NASA astronauts to 50.

Average age of the group is 33.3 years. Average number of college years 5.8, and average flight time is 2,714 hours, of which 1,925 hours is jet time. Two of the new astronauts have doctorates. Two are single.

Four civilians are among those selected. Of the remainder, 7 are Air Force officers, 6 are Navy Officers, and 2 are Marine Corps officers.

They include:

Vance D. Brand, 34, an engineering test pilot for Lockheed assigned to the West German F-104G Flight Test Center at Istres, France. Brand, his wife and 4 children live at Martigues, France.

Lt. John S. Bull, USN, 31, a test pilot at the Naval Air Station, Patuxent River, Maryland. Bull, his wife and son live on the base.

Maj. Gerald P. Carr, USMC, 33, Tests Director Section, Marine Corps Air Facility, Santa Ana, California. Carr, his wife and 6 children live in Santa Ana.

Capt. Charles M. Duke, Jr., USAF, 30, instructor at Aerospace Research Pilot School, Edwards Air Force Base, California. Duke, his wife and one son live in Edwards, Calif.

Capt. Walden J. Eckhardt, USAF, 32, experimental test pilot, Edwards AFB, Calif. Eckhardt and his wife live in Edwards.

Capt. Joe H. Engle, USAF, 33, aerospace research flight test officer assigned as project pilot for

X-15, Edwards AFB, Calif. Engle, his wife and two children live in Edwards.

Lt. Cdr. Ronald E. Evans, USN, 32, on sea duty in the Pacific. His wife and two children live in San Diego, Calif.

Maj. Edward G. Givens, Jr., USAF, 36, project officer at the NASA Manned Spacecraft Center for the Astronaut Maneuvering Unit (Gemini experiment D-12). Givens, his wife and two children live in Seabrook (El Lago), Texas.

Fred W. Haise, Jr., 32, NASA project pilot at Flight Research Center, Edwards, Calif. Haise, his wife and 3 children live in Lancaster, Calif.

Dr. Don L. Lind, 35, physicist at NASA Goddard Space flight Center, Greenbelt, Maryland. Lind, his wife and 5 children live in Silver Spring, Md.

Capt. Jack R. Lousma, USMC, 30, operational pilot at Marine Air Station, Cherry Point, North Carolina. Lousma, his wife and one son live in Newport, N.C.

Lt. Thomas K. Mattingly, USN, 30, student in Aerospace Research Pilot School, Edwards AFB, Calif. He is single and lives on base.

Lt. Bruce McCandless, III, USN, 28, working toward a doctorate in electrical engineering at Stanford University. McCandless, his wife and two children live in Mountain View, Calif.

Lt. Cdr. Edgar D. Mitchell, USN, 35, student in Aerospace Research Pilot School, Edwards AFB, Calif. He has a doctor of science degree from Massachusetts Institute of Technology. Mitchell, hs wife and two daughters live in Torrance, Calif.

Maj. William R. Pogue, USAF, 36, instructor in Aerospace Research Pilot School, Edwards AFB, Calif. Pogue, his wife and 3 children live at Edwards.

Capt. Stuart A. Roosa, USAF, 32, experimental test pilot at Edwards AFB, Calif. Roosa, his wife and 4 children live in Edwards.

John L. Swigert, Jr., 34, engineering test pilot for North American Aviation, Inc. He is single and lives in South Gate, Calif.

Lt. Cdr. Paul J. Weitz, USN, 33, squadron operations officer. Weitz, his wife and two children live on Oak Harbor, Washington.

Capt. Alfred M. Worden, USAF, 34, instructor at Aerospace Research Pilot School, Edwards AFB, Calif. Worden, his wife and two daughters live in Edwards.

Recruiting of the new astronauts began Sept. 10, 1965. A total of 351 submitted applications, of which 159 met basic requirements. Of that number, 100 were military, 59 civilian. For consideration, applicants must have been a United States citizen; no taller than 6 feet; born on or after Dec. 1, 1929; have a bachelor degree in engineering, physical or biological sciences; and have acquired 1000 hours jet pilot time or have graduated from an armed forces test pilot school.

—)—

Printed in Great Britain
by Amazon.co.uk, Ltd.,
Marston Gate.